LESSONS IN
ANOTHER LANGUAGE

ALSO BY MEGAN STAFFEL

A Length of Wire and Other Stories
She Wanted Something Else
The Notebook of Lost Things

LESSONS IN
Another Language

A Novella and Stories

Megan Staffel

FOUR WAY BOOKS
TRIBECA

Please direct all inquiries to:
Editorial Office
Four Way Books
POB 535, Village Station
New York, NY 10014
www.fourwaybooks.com

Library of Congress Cataloging-in-Publication Data
Staffel, Megan, 1952-
Lessons in another language : a novella and stories / Megan Staffel.
    p. cm.
ISBN 978-1-935536-00-0 (pbk. : alk. paper)
I. Title. PS3569.T16L45 2010
813'.54--dc22

                    2009029541

This book is manufactured in the United States of America
and printed on acid-free paper.

Four Way Books is a not-for-profit literary press. We are grateful for the assistance we receive
from individual donors, public arts agencies, and private foundations.

 This publication is made possible with public funds
from the National Endowment for the Arts

 and from the New York State Council on the Arts,
a state agency.

Distributed by University Press of New England
One Court Street, Lebanon, NH 03766

[clmp] We are a proud member of
the Council of Literary Magazines and Presses.

for Graham

CONTENTS

LESSONS IN
ANOTHER LANGUAGE

The Linguist

Nathan Bogmore stood at the front door in his pajamas, squinting into the afternoon, wishing he could simply get back under the sheets and forget everything. It was 1967, and Nathan was fourteen years old. He was at the age when sleep was necessary not for rest or rejuvenation, but courage. It blunted the indignities of a family vacation and whisked him off to another place. That it was a place he couldn't remember once he woke up didn't matter. Maybe it was not even a place of longitude and latitude, but a celebration he returned to every night, a Nathan Bogmorian Convention that was a singing of praises and admirations, a sending, to him, of assurances that he was right about everything.

His mother called it a working vacation. And a working vacation was a dubious and drawn-out affair, because in his family work meant creating art. At that very moment Nathan could hear his father moving around in the ceramic studio he'd set up in the garage, and in the direction of the main house, down the road a quarter mile, there was the sound of drumming as the modern dance troupe did their warm-ups on the lawn. His mother was painting in her studio at the smaller cottage, and his sister, a girl two years his junior who was named Genevieve on her birth certificate, but called Jimmy by family and friends, was either dancing with the troupe or helping Mack water the trees that had just been planted on the edge of his property.

So much creativity saturating the already sticky climate of the day only made it harder for Nathan to resist the urge to go back to bed. To burst into these goings-on at that late hour would take nothing less than a powerful effort, and Nathan wasn't sure he wanted to go to all the trouble. He looked down at his bare toes. He looked into the woods directly across from the cottage where they were staying and saw a bunch of trees. What saved him, what saved him every time, was hunger. So he turned around, let the screen door slam shut behind him, and went into the kitchen to find breakfast.

The school year had gone badly for Nathan, and even though it was summer vacation, he should have been up hours earlier studying his French. He'd managed to pass math and English, but he had failed French. To go on to the second level, he had to take summer school. The session was free, paid for by the Board of Education, and it ran for eight weeks in July and August, meaning that the Bogmores' peripatetic habits would be curtailed. When the letter arrived from the principal, all of that was resolved. No wanderings through New England, no week-long stays at the Jersey shore. Because of Nathan, they would have to endure the whole stretch of summer right there in humid Philadelphia.

It was finalized. The box on the letter was checked, and Nathan was enrolled in French camp at Temple University. He would take the Germantown Avenue trolley to the Broad Street subway and the subway to the Temple stop. He would not pay attention to the smell of urine in the underground tunnel or the trash whipping along the dusty street in the hot wind. He would simply attend class and come home. It would be a long and boring summer, but in Nathan's mind it was a just punishment, matching in its dullness the level of intrigue he had felt at the start of the year when a slick and dangerous confidence, a confidence born in his dreams, had whisked him far beyond the meaninglessness of ninth grade.

But. And in the Bogmore family that *but* was everything. Nothing was secure against it. It could wedge into any resolution and blow it apart.

The but in this case was Phyllis. She invited the entire family to stay in the cottage on Mack's summer place in Connecticut. There was a large room in a smaller cottage for Judy, Nathan's mother, to paint in, and a very suitable garage space where Stuart, Nathan's father, could have a kiln and a potter's wheel. All in exchange for a few hours every morning helping Mack plant some trees.

Judy had been delighted. She told Phyllis they would love to do it and she'd call back the next day with a definite answer. That evening at dinner she related the proposal to the rest of the family. Saved from a summer of Hell, his mother was as giddy as a little girl. It made Nathan particularly joyful to know that he was going to be the one to destroy her plans.

"I failed French, remember? Summer school?"

"Nathan, don't be sarcastic."

She was ladling soup into bowls. That was the period of the one-pot meals. So she could have a longer day in the studio, she cooked chicken, beans, and vegetables on the weekend and made soup from it all week long, varying the ingredients so it wouldn't get boring. By the end of the week, everything was so mushy she just threw it into the blender, and Friday's soup was a brown purée. You could still find bits of carrot and chicken, which Nathan took the trouble to do, because he liked food to be distinct.

"Oh shit, I had forgotten. You're sure you failed French? The grades aren't in yet, are they? Maybe you managed to squeak through."

Nathan went to the desk and pulled out the letter the principal had mailed to them the week before. "It says it right here. I failed."

"Wouldn't it be wonderful if Mack and Phyllis had a place in France? Then it would solve everything. You're having trouble because you don't know what the language sounds like. What you need is to be surrounded by French. Then you'd just fall into it, automatically."

"Automatically," Jimmy mimicked. His beautiful sister thrust out her nonexistent hips and gave him a sultry glance.

"If Mack and Phyllis had a place in France, we would have to row across the Atlantic in a bathtub. That's about all we could afford," his father said, slapping his mother on the rear end. She told him to leave her alone and go do something useful. To Jimmy she said, "Go play the piano, why don't you." Then, with music filling the kitchen, she made Nathan sit down at the table. "We're going to find a way to make it work. Because a summer in the country, and you can bet any amount of money that Mack and Phyllis's place is really exquisite, because I know them, they never do anything halfway, is healthier for you children than a summer cooped up in a hot, dirty city. Believe me."

Nathan had looked at her silently. "Cooped up" wouldn't have been the words he would have used to describe it. He saw it as release, a summer of roaming the streets, a summer of independence.

—⟨ↄ⟩

They went. Judy wrote a letter to the principal unenrolling Nathan in French camp. She put an ad in the paper in Danbury, Connecticut, for a French tutor, and the second day after they arrived at the compound that sat at the end of a dirt road, hidden in a lush and tangled forest, Mademoiselle Bruneau puttered down the long driveway that linked their cottage to the main house, bumping over the stones in a peculiar-looking car that he discovered later was called a Citroën.

"*Bonjour Nathan, comment vas-tu? Tu vas bien?*" She spoke to him immediately, getting right to business, not even waiting to shut the rusted door on her car. When she leaned into the back seat to get her paper, books, and pencil case, Nathan had a view of middle-aged buttocks packed into a tight skirt, and imagining her pale and meaty nakedness, led her to the cottage. That whole first lesson he stared at her face, noticing the layer of powder, the streak of rouge. She was not discouraged by his inattention, and as her light, cheerful voice spoke the phrases she wanted him to learn, French not only seemed to be as pale and middle-aged as she was, but as perfumed. *"Comment t'appelles-tu? Tu es Nathan?"*

"*Oui*," he said lamely and followed her around the cottage as she stuck labels on all of their furniture. On the door to his parents' room it said, "*le père, la mère*." On the door to Jimmy's room it said, "*la sœur*." On his door it said, "*le frère*."

For the next week, as he swam and ate and walked the road between their cottage and the main house, his mind was occupied with French. Once he got out of bed, he would find himself making the effort. *Le bateau* was the word he thought of as he and Jimmy pushed the rowboat into the shiny, black pond that sat at the bottom of the enormous lawn, and when Jimmy was at the oars and it drifted too close to the willows, forcing them to duck under the trailing leaves, he thought, *l'arbre*. When they entered the darkness underneath the trees, where insects hung in clouds and frogs they couldn't see plopped into the murky water, all that circled around in his mind was *l'eau*. And when Jimmy would hold the boat still, jamming her oar into the soft mud so they would have to stay there and endure the mosquitoes, he glared at her and thought, *la sœur*. Even though the clammy feeling of the place made his hands sweat, he thought, *il est midi*. Because he didn't know how to add qualities, his mind lost its adjectives and started to focus on the thing in its neutral state, in its perfect beingness. Of course, there was the time he got so angry at her he kicked the oar out of her hand. It flew up and splattered them both with mud. That gave them the idea. The next time, they rowed under the willows purposely and used the oar like a shovel to scoop up the soft mud, which *la sœur* patted on her face and legs and arms until she was covered. Nathan didn't like touching the mud, so he painted his face and that was all. Then they rowed back to the dock and lay down in the sun to let it dry. But it didn't dry brown. It dried blue and smelly.

"Haven't you been smelling something?" Jimmy asked, suddenly sitting upright.

"You," he answered. "La sewer." He started to laugh. "La sewer!"

She dove into the water, staying under until the far side of the pond, where she popped up, her face clean and white, her long brown hair shiny with wetness. He dove in after her, because the smell was pretty terrible and he had been thinking about all of the frog poop that must have settled into the very mud he'd patted on his cheeks.

"La sewer!" he shouted. "La sewer!" He tried to make her angry, but she only said in her superior tone, "Oh shut up. You're such a baby."

"I'm a *garçon*," he shouted, kicking water into her face.

But she was a better swimmer than he was, and no amount of splashing would make her falter. She was also a better diver. And she could play the piano and improvise with the dancers in the troupe, who were also in residence, and like his parents, planted trees in the morning and lived like guests on the estate the rest of the day. They loved Jimmy and predicted a career for her in modern dance.

Somehow, even though she was two years younger, she had moved far ahead of him. She had figured out all the connections, so that she could move from one accomplishment to another, never even looking like she was working very hard at anything. She had whole strings of connections, while he went from one simple noun to another, doomed to the dullness of single words.

Dinners at the main house were formal. First there were cocktails in the living room. The evening sun (*le soleil*) hit the bottles of booze like a dagger, making them glisten at the center of the room. Nathan and Jimmy were each served a small glass of sherry.

Jimmy drank hers in little sips as she played the piano. All she played, all that summer, was Beethoven's "Für Elise." She'd been able to get it to sound pretty good on their out-of-tune upright at home, but on the grand piano in the living room of the big house on Mack and Phyllis's estate, it was urgent and insinuating, and Nathan was amazed every time he heard it. How could it be that simply following a bunch of stupid notes she could make him have such feelings? It was as though Beethoven had sailed back through the ether with a message just for him. So he listened. But the exasperating thing was that Jimmy liked to play when there was an audience. Her eyes would get a glazed-over look, and she'd sway in and out, her long white fingers like spider legs arched over the keys.

Nathan stayed in the living room, studying the design in the oriental carpet, trying to match it to the design on the sofa. Or he smelled the odor of old fires that wafted out of the enormous fireplace and tried to balance it with the bits of conversation or the fan moving above their heads, black blades whipping the air into a steamy froth. *La conversation.* He couldn't figure out why any of it mattered. Or if it did. And if it didn't, he wanted to know why they bothered. For instance, what was the point of playing music and making someone feel out of control? He went from the bowl of black olives, to the bowl of green olives, to the tray of cheese and crackers, to the bowls of baby corn and tiny gherkins, taking a sample at each stop.

"There's my boy!" Mack slapped him so soundly between the shoulders he almost spit out the olive pit he had been exploring with his tongue. "Hey!" It was a hearty sound meaning nothing. "How're those French lessons?"

"Fine," he said.

"Well, parley voo that."

"*Bien.*"

"Good boy! I'll tell you, a man can never learn too much. Could be that foreign language will one day save his life. Bet you didn't know I was stationed near Paris at the end of the war. Hey! How're those olives?"

"Did you kill anyone?"

"Never had to. Now tell me, if it were up to you, which ones do you think are best, the black or the green? Give me your honest opinion."

Mack leaned in close to him as though he really wanted to know, and gazing into his light blue eyes, Nathan saw a flicker of something, a shadow passing where a shadow shouldn't have passed, because the man's eyes were so blue and filled with light. Yet something dark had opened up inside them and then closed just as suddenly. There on the rosy, liver-spotted face, something in the eyes, something he shouldn't have seen. And Mack knew that he'd seen it. *Le secret.*

Estella rang the dinner bell, and they filed into the dining room. Jimmy got up from the piano and joined Nathan at the table. They were placed together between Erik, the drummer, and Molly, a dancer who always wore long flouncy skirts with petticoats underneath them. She also wore mostly unbuttoned blouses and was haphazard about the way she leaned over. For Nathan, meals were a series of hurried glances down the ravine between her breasts.

"Lovely, lovely, lovely," Phyllis sang out, clapping her hands. "The table looks lovely, Estella!"

"Thank you ma'am," Estella said as she came in with a platter of roasted chicken.

"And it smells heavenly. And Jimmy, your playing sounds more wonderful every day. Aren't we lucky mortals? I'm so glad we're all here together, working and making art, and I feel so lucky to have Mack, and Mack is so lucky to have money." She pouted a little and asked, "You don't mind my saying that, do you, sweetheart?"

In a voice made gravelly by years of smoking, Mack answered to the table at large: "As a businessman it is my duty to be sensitive to the plight of artists. The sacrifices you people make enrich the lives of us common folk. You show us beauty, you show us truth. And when I had the great good luck to meet Phyllis, well, that was when my life took a very surprising turn."

"Isn't he a wonderful man?" Phyllis asked. "I'm so glad I married you."

"She married me just for my money," Mack said and then laughed.

"I did, sweetheart, I did. And then I fell head over heels."

"Let's have a toast to Mack and Phyllis, who made it possible for all of us to be together." *Le père* said that. He took it upon himself to be master of ceremonies, the liaison between the nobility and the peasants.

"As long as you plant those trees!" Mack cried out.

"And make art and make dances," Phyllis added. Then she said, "We are so lucky, all of us, to be here at this wonderful place. And to have your delicious food, Estella."

"Thank you ma'am."

She was stopping between each of them, holding the heavy platter of chicken with one hand and serving with the other. Her skin against her crisply starched uniform was a warm brown, and as she moved from person to person her posture stayed stooped. By the time she came between Nathan and Molly her arm was so unsteady the platter was shaking. Nathan stated his choices quickly, so she could move on. That was how he, the one who existed in a world of simple middle-aged nouns, tried to help her out. But then he noticed that the shaking stopped when she was between Jimmy and Erik, and he saw that Jimmy had put her own hand under the platter to give Estella's hand a rest. She didn't say anything, and Estella didn't say anything either, and when she moved on to serve the next person, the platter started to shake again.

Erik, the only male in the dance troupe, had straight black

hair and an overly serious expression. He wore black tights and a black tee shirt whether they were rehearsing or not, and he seemed particularly solicitous of Jimmy, which made Nathan jealous, because Molly ignored him except to lean over and let him gaze down her cleavage.

"How are the trees coming along, Mack?" Erik asked across the table. "Are we on schedule?"

"A bit behind," Mack said. "Tomorrow, I'd like to start at six o'clock." Nathan looked up and saw the butterfly wing close suddenly in Mack's eye. "We could use a strong kid like you, Nathan. Can you pull him out of bed, Stuart? He could handle the water cart. Maybe Jimmy could help Estella in the kitchen."

"Can't I plant trees too? I'm just as strong as Nathan."

"Can you make use of her?" Mack asked Estella, who was coming around with a platter of rice.

"Sure thing, boss. You get here at six o'clock, young lady, and I'll put you to work." When she smiled at Jimmy, Nathan saw dark gaps in her mouth from missing teeth.

Mack was planting Russian olives along the borders of his two hundred acres. It was a small ornamental tree with tiny oval leaves. Barbed-wire fencing would have been faster and cheaper, but Mack grew up on a huge ranch in the West, and he wanted the illusion of infinite space, but for practical reasons he needed to know where his boundaries were. The tree planting was slow work so Phyllis, Mack's third wife and a former member of a modern dance troupe, conceived the plan of inviting her friends from New York City. She thought of Stuart and Judy in Philadelphia when she realized that the smallest cottage would make an ideal studio for a painter and the garage of the larger cottage would be adequate for Stuart's ceramics. The dancers stayed in the guest rooms in the main house, and she gave the cottages to the Bogmores.

The next morning, Nathan was up at five o'clock with everyone else. He put on a grumpy act because he assumed it would be expected, but really, he was pleased to be awake when the sky was just getting light and the woods behind the cottage were full of singing birds. He did what he was supposed to do—he got dressed and ate a bowl of cereal—secretly watching himself go through the routine.

Le père was full of energy, *la mère* was quiet, *la sœur* kept bumping into him as they walked down the road to the main house. Nathan didn't bump back. There wasn't any need to engage with any of them. Everything around him was shouting, the grass, the sky, the black-eyed Susans growing at the side of the road, and he looked at each thing and in his mind hammered the offender with its French name till it shut up under the pressure. It was amazing how the world could be ordered and controlled. Even *les oiseaux*, the birds. They chirped in a sedate manner now; the wildflowers weren't so brazen. The brilliant blue sky clouded over, and French was no longer so female and perfumed. He'd made the language his.

Jimmy went into the big house, the screen door snapping shut behind her, and Nathan followed his parents into the barn, where the dancers were already loading the truck with trees. The Russian olives were small and easy to lift, and they'd swing them up to the bed of the truck, standing them on their burlap-

15

wrapped dirt balls. They loaded twenty-five trees, and then they hooked up the trailer for the water cart.

The screen door snapped again, and Mack came out of the house in work clothes and a cowboy hat. He slapped Nathan on the shoulder and then showed him how to fill the empty drum from the large tank on the truck. Water was going to be Nathan's responsibility. When the water cart was empty, he'd have to fill it again from the tank on the big truck.

Stuart rode up front with Mack, and everyone else walked. The truck went the same pace that they did, smashing down weeds and saplings as it crossed the field and climbed the hill to the spot where they had finished the day before.

His mother was lagging behind, talking to Molly, but then she caught up with Nathan. "Isn't it glorious?"

Phyllis always said "glorious." The sky was glorious, the food was glorious, the conversation was glorious. "It's okay," Nathan replied. It was essential, always, to lock his feelings away.

"It hasn't rained yet," she added. "Mack wants it to, because the trees really need it. I do too. I need the day off."

"Yeah, but we only have to work till ten thirty."

"It's hard though. You wait and see." She took off her work gloves and held out her hands. "See these?" She pointed to fleshy bumps on her palm. "Calluses. You try shoveling for a couple of hours."

"I'm not going to shovel. I'm going to pull the water cart."

His mother didn't even acknowledge the challenging tone of his voice. She took off her canvas hat and wiped her forehead. "Even now it's getting hot. Nathan, you didn't wear a hat."

"I'll be okay."

"With the sun beating down on you, you'll get really tired."

"I thought we were going to be in the woods."

"Right, but there'll be flies."

"I'll be fine," he said testily.

Part of the excitement he'd been feeling that year came from understanding the power of his body. He didn't get cold and he didn't get hot. Flies didn't bother him. Shoveling, if he had to do it, wouldn't bother him either, because he could stand almost anything. Hadn't he gone through the entire winter wearing nothing heavier than a sweatshirt? Even during their one snow-storm.

Molly caught up to *la mère*, and sending Nathan a glance, put her hand on his mother's arm. "I'd love to come to your studio sometime and see what you're doing."

"Oh gosh, really? I'm not ready yet. I'm just getting started."

"What are you working on?

"Well, I thought I'd do a series of paintings of the pond. In fact, I think I'm just going to paint the pond all summer."

Nathan could tell that Molly thought that was a stupid idea, because she said, "Really?" in a way that sounded false.

His mother didn't notice. "It changes all the time. In the morning if it's sunny it looks one way, in the evening, it's all dark and mysterious. I saw a deer drinking at it the other evening."

"Wow!" Molly said. "I'll have to pay better attention."

"I've never lived in the country," *la mère* went on, "and every-thing just seems like a miracle. A raccoon, a deer, even the way the squirrels chatter at you from the trees."

"Tell me something, are you enjoying it?"

"Oh heavens yes. Anything to get out of the city. To breathe such clean air." She looked at Molly, and not seeing any sign of agreement, went on. "All the glorious shades of green, the grass, the trees."

"Do you think it's fair that we should be doing this back-breaking work? An hour or two I'd be happy to put in. But four and a half hours is exhausting, and frankly, our rehearsals aren't going well because everyone's so tired. You have to be really fo-cused for modern dance. Intention has to inform every move-ment, and what we've been doing lately has just felt blurred."

"I know it's hard, but Mack's depending on us."

"I'd be happy to do it for a short while."

"And they treat us so well. That wonderful food and a whole cottage to use as a studio."

"Our studio is the lawn, and it slopes," Molly said discontent-edly. "You have a cottage to live in, and we all have these rather small rooms, and mine is right above Mack and Phyllis's, and he's got the TV on late every night. I don't know if the man has in-somnia or what, but I can't sleep with that insipid noise, and then with this work so early in the morning . . ."

"Excuse me," *la mère* said, "I want to catch Nathan for a minute. Can we talk again later?"

"Of course we can. And remember, I really would like to see those pond paintings when you're ready to show them."

"Thanks," his mother called, steering him off to the side, right behind the tailpipe. Nathan got a lungful of smoke and coughed it out noisily.

"Are you all right, sweetheart? Listen, I've been wanting to ask you, how's French?"

"Fine."

"Well, say something to me."

"*Le frère.*"

"Let's see, that's brother. Gosh, it's been so long. Well good. Can you say something else?"

"*La sœur.*"

"Oh, I know what that is. The sister."

"*Très belle.*"

"Oh yes, I'm starting to remember. Very beautiful. Your sister *is* very beautiful, isn't she? But you're very handsome. Let's see. *Le garçon est* . . . I don't know the word for handsome."

He didn't either. It wasn't a word, even in English, he thought about. Probably because he didn't care if he was handsome or not. Power was what he wanted. But it wasn't power like strong muscles. Another kind of power. A power that lifted him above all of the petty problems of his existence, like flies and hot sun and the necessity to learn another language, to a place somewhere in the atmosphere where all surfaces were smooth, and logic was the supreme order, not feelings.

Even though he hadn't done well in math that year, he had appreciated the systems. All you had to do was set down a system, and then you could use it to answer any number of problems, and each time, if you stuck to the system, you'd get the right answer.

Nathan heard Mack shift the truck into a lower gear as the hill got steeper. The back wheels slipped in the soft dirt, and a couple of the trees fell over.

"When's your next lesson?"

"She's coming this afternoon."

"Well, you pay really good attention. Just let go of English and try to melt into the French, okay? If you resist, it will be that much harder."

"*Oui, maman.*"

"That's my sweetheart. Look, we're getting close. That's where we stopped yesterday."

Mack parked the truck on a level spot, and Nathan's father jumped out and opened the tailgate. Everyone took a shovel. His father went off with a tape measure and marked the place for each tree and then cut away the undergrowth to clear a spot for the hole. Nathan watched him, waiting for Mack to give him his instructions. Soon, he heard the dry sounds of shovels scratching against the hard earth. There wasn't even any dew to wet the surface. The dirt they shoveled up was a light brown, mixed with rock, and only when they were down a foot or more did the soil turn damp.

"First, we're going to fill the water cart." Mack didn't look at him, just stooped down and undid the clamps holding the water cart on the trailer. "You wheel it over to the hose. That's right. See, it's easy to push when it's empty. But you're a strong boy, so it won't matter when it gets a little heavy. You must work out. I've seen those muscles you have. All right now . . . "

Mack uncoiled the hose from the bed of the truck. It was hooked to a fifty-gallon drum they had filled at the house that morning. "See, you position it like this," he said, putting the nozzle into the top of the cart. Water ran noisily into the empty tank. "Now, you have to watch it, because if you don't turn the spigot off when it's full, the water will just spill out, and we can't let that happen. This is the only water we've got, and all these little trees, they're depending on you, Nathan. They don't get water, they die.

And I know you don't want that to happen. Now, takes a while to dig the holes. Hasn't rained in three weeks and the ground's like cement. Want to see something? Hey! Come over here."

The kind of power Nathan dreamed of was uninvolved power. He might have admired the way Mack ordered everyone around, if he hadn't felt a hint of cruelty. Nathan's power came out of a disinterested involvement, and since logic was its operative, it didn't ever have to manipulate. He followed Mack into a grove of trees. Mack said they were ash.

"Look at this." Mack had stopped in front of a tree. He pointed to scratches on the bark, places where something had rubbed the bark down to the yellow wood underneath. "That's made by a buck sharpening his antlers."

"How'd you find it?"

"Oh, just happened to see it. Yup, a young buck, horny as Hell, rubbing his antlers. Go ahead, Nathan, touch it."

Nathan reached out and touched the damp scar.

"Now that's something! You stick with Mack and you'll see some things. A horny young buck, well." The cowboy hat was back on his head. "Us boys need to stick together." In the leaf-dappled sunlight, caught with Mack between the trees, Nathan felt his hands get moist. The butterfly wings were completely open in the older man's eyes, and Nathan knew he shouldn't look at them closely, even though he could tell, in a side glance, that the designs were beautiful.

That afternoon, he sat at the kitchen table with Mademoiselle Bruneau. "*Le lac, le fleuve.*" He repeated after her, hearing the easy glide of the words in his mind and knowing they came out halted and sloppy. "*La maison, l'homme, l'arbre.*" Those last two he thought he said well.

"*Très bien!*" Mademoiselle said, clapping her hands, her bracelets jingling. "*Nathan, s'il te plaît, un verre d'eau.*"

He sat a moment, trying to figure it out.

"*Un verre d'eau, s'il te plaît.*"

Suddenly, he understood, but he stood up so quickly the chair fell backward. His face went red, because Mademoiselle was laughing. "*Maladroit,*" she said.

He had a pretty good idea what that meant. He placed the glass on the table, and she lifted it eagerly to take a sip. "Delicious water. Everyone should drink eight glasses of water a day. Do you know why?"

"No, Mademoiselle."

"Water lubricates all the systems. It does the same thing in your body as oil does in an engine. Do you know what oil does in an engine?"

"It lets all the different parts move."

"That's right. You're a very smart boy. I bet you can't wait till you can drive, can you?"

"I can wait."

"*Mon dieu!* A boy who isn't anxious to drive! How very unusual!"

The truth was that he hadn't even thought about driving.

"All right, back to *le français.* Now, in our first week, you've learned many nouns. It's time for review. When I say each word, I want you to repeat it after me, write it down, spelling it correctly, and then tell me what it means."

They spent the whole lesson making a list, and when they were done, there were sixty-two nouns. He knew about half of them by heart. The rest he would have to study.

"Next week, I will give you a test."

"A test?"

"A test. And I expect it to be one hundred percent correct. And if it is, we will move on to verbs."

"Mademoiselle, I don't think they give tests in summer school."

"They most certainly do, and therefore we will have a test here." She unzipped her pencil case and took out a freshly sharpened pencil.

"Mademoiselle, what is the word for suspicion?"

"Suspicion? That is an English word I don't know."

"If I am afraid that a person is trying to do something secretly, that's a suspicion."

"Ah, *soupçon!* Should we add that one to the list? You are an unusual boy, Nathan. My nephew, who is one year younger than you, can't wait till he can start to drive, and rocket or airplane or battleship, those are the words he wants me to teach him." She wrote the time and day of their next meeting, then put her pencil back in the case and stood up, her bracelets jingling. "Good boy, study your words, drink eight glasses of water a day, and obey your parents." He walked her to her car, noticing the way the gravel driveway made her teeter in her high heels.

When Jimmy came back from the main house, they fixed themselves big glasses of chocolate milk for lunch and were drinking it on the front steps when their father walked up from the garage.

"Hi kids," he said nonchalantly. "Having fun?"

Jimmy said yup, Nathan said yes.

"Is your mother home yet?"

"She's still at her studio."

"So, what are you two doing this afternoon?"

"Hey Dad," Nathan called, "do you want to come fishing?" They hadn't done anything together, just the three of them, in a long time.

"Fishing?"

Nathan could tell *le père* was trying to think of an excuse to get out of it.

"Are there fishing rods?"

"Whole bunch of them in the barn."

"Well, I've got to fire a kiln this afternoon. Can we go another day? I'm not going to have time to do anything today except jump in for a quick dip. Why don't you and Jimmy go fishing."

Their father disappeared into the house to make himself some lunch. They stayed on the step, listening to the sounds coming from the kitchen. They knew he was making his customary peanut butter and banana sandwich and washing a piece of fruit. They also knew it was hopeless to try and get him to come fishing. They didn't say that, they didn't have to. It was enough just to be on the step together, caught in the sound of their father's lunch-making activities. The resentment they both felt slowly evaporated into the heavy trill of the insects.

"Know what I think?" Jimmy was digging her toes into the warm gravel. "I bet they didn't want kids. I bet we were accidents."

"I might have been an accident. But then they realized it wasn't so bad, so they decided to have you."

"Yeah, they wanted me, and they only kept you because they couldn't send you back."

"Maybe. Want to go fishing?"

"I ain't never done it before."

Their father, who was coming out the front door with a sandwich in his hand said, "Jimmy, there's no reason to talk like that. In this family we speak correctly, am I right?"

"You're right," she said. She pushed her hair out of her eyes and looked up at Nathan. "Teach me how to do it, okay?"

"Sure," he said. But he'd only done it once or twice himself, and that was a long time ago.

The two of them walked down the road to the main house. Jimmy had put her sneakers back on, but Nathan had taken his off and was walking barefoot to toughen up the soles of his feet. In the gloomy coolness of the barn he saw a bunch of fishing rods propped against the back wall. He took down two and handed Jimmy a tackle box he saw in the corner. Then he rummaged around in the gardening shed till he found a trowel.

"What's that for?"

"Bait."

"What're we going to use for bait?"

"I'm going to use worms. You can use whatever you want to use."

By the house, they could hear the music from the lawn where the dancers were rehearsing. When they walked around to the other side, they could see the three women twirling around in brightly colored skirts and then, one by one, diving down onto the grass, each skirt opening like a fan around them.

25

"Don't they look like flowers?" Jimmy said in awe.

Nathan thought they looked like girls doing something stupid. Erik came prancing between them, the drum hanging from a shoulder strap so he could drum and dance at the same time.

Nathan kept on going. "So what're you going to do?" he asked when Jimmy caught up.

"Do the worms have to get killed?"

"How else are you going to get them onto the hook?"

"I don't want to kill a worm."

"Fine. Fish with raisins."

"Fish don't eat raisins."

"Right, they don't." Nathan squatted in the shade of the willows, digging in the dirt. Even there it was dry. The worms had to tunnel down deep to find any moisture. He dug till he reached soft black earth and picked out five big fat ones. He closed his fist around them and walked over to the dock and, before they could wiggle away, cut each one into thirds. He left the pieces in a clump under the strong sun. Then he took a fishing rod and poked the hook through one of the worm pieces. Stuff came oozing out around the hook, but Nathan didn't notice. Jimmy had come over to watch. "You want me to put one on your hook too?"

"I don't want to go fishing."

"Okay, then all of these worms are going to waste, because I can't use them all."

"Well, you were stupid for cutting them all up."

"You were stupid for saying you were going to come fishing if you weren't going to let me put a worm on your hook."

"I'm going to get some raisins."

"But you said yourself, fish don't eat raisins."

"Maybe they do." She ran off toward the main house, and he watched her make a wide arc around the dancers and get swallowed into the shadows of the patio. When she came back, she put a raisin on her hook and cast the way he had done, her line plunking easily into the center of the pond.

"How'd you learn how to cast like that?"

"Estella told me."

"Estella knows how to fish?"

"She doesn't fish for fish. She fishes for spirits. The pond goes to the underworld, and if you want to fish you have to ask the spirits if you can join them."

"Is that what you did?"

She nodded, and when he looked at her skeptically she said, "You don't have to ask them out loud. You just ask them in your head."

"If you say so." He was floating at the top of the sky, where nothing Jimmy said had any meaning and where the fact that they sat there, the two of them, and fished all afternoon, he with pieces of worm and she with raisins, and caught nothing at all, and didn't even feel a tug, didn't matter. It was summer, there was nothing to do, and all he knew was how to go from one thing to another thing, and there was no way that he could see to make any of it string together.

At dinner that night, Jimmy didn't sit next to him. She was helping Estella in the kitchen. When their mother noticed her absence she said, "Nathan, where's Jimmy?"

Though it would have been easy enough to tell her, he didn't

27

want to, so he pretended he didn't know. Just then, Jimmy came out with bowls of soup.

"You're serving?"

Jimmy nodded yes, happily. She moved around the table, leaning over each person's right shoulder and placing a bowl of soup in front of them.

"When are you going to eat?"

"I'm going to eat in the kitchen," Jimmy said.

"But I don't see you all day long. I really want you to eat with us." She looked at their father. "Honey, don't you agree?"

"She should do what she wants."

When Jimmy came out next with a bowl of freshly grated cheese, which she offered to each guest for their soup, his mother said, "Jimmy, don't you want to eat with us?"

"Estella's teaching me how to cook," Jimmy said proudly.

When she went back to the kitchen, *la mère* turned to Mack and Phyllis and said, "I hardly see her. I really want to have her with us at dinner."

"This is part of her job," Mack said. "You'll have her all night, Judy."

"And look at her," Phyllis added. "She's so happy to have responsibility."

That night Mack invited them all into the living room for after-dinner drinks. Nathan and Jimmy each got their usual sherry. Jimmy was heading to the piano when Phyllis said, "Jimmy dear, you know we love to hear you play, but tonight I wanted to put on some records. Just for a change."

"Come here, sweetheart," their mother called. "I want to talk to you." She held out her arms, and when Jimmy came over their mother gave her a long hug. "So what did you do this morning with Estella?"

"I helped her chop up vegetables."

"That was all?"

"She showed me how to make a pie crust."

"You mean that delicious pie crust was yours?"

"With Estella's help."

"Oh honey, I'm so proud of you. It was so light and flaky. Really terrific. When we get back home, will you teach me? I'm such a klutz at baking."

Suddenly, dance music filled the living room. Phyllis grabbed Mack and the two of them swung around, arm in arm, like people in a movie. Erik chose Natalie and they swooped and twirled dramatically. *Le père* and *la mère* shuffled around in each other's arms with smiles plastered on their faces, and Molly came over to Nathan. "Put down your glass and I'll teach you how to do it."

He froze up. How could his body fit against hers with all of that stuff in the way? But Molly seemed unconcerned. She put his left arm around her waist, grabbed his right hand, and steered him into the center of the room. "Just do what I do. And relax. You feel as stiff as a piece of wood."

All Nathan wanted was to get back to his glass of wine. Her perfume was suffocating him and the proximity of so much female made him nervous.

"Loosen up," Molly whispered. "I'm not going to bite you. Now, lift your arm. I'm going to twirl around under it. See. That wasn't so hard, was it? Now, you twirl."

29

He wobbled around and managed to find her on the return.

"Okay. A little stiff, because you're moving like a robot, but not bad. You know what you should do? You should come out on the lawn with us. Try some improvising. You're not trusting your body. And you need to learn to trust it. Tomorrow afternoon, why don't you come out?"

The song finally ended, and Molly released him. Nathan returned to his glass, but afraid that someone else would make him dance, he didn't stay in the living room. He went into the kitchen looking for Jimmy. But the kitchen was dark. Still holding his glass, he went outside. There was a soft breeze, a scent of freshly cut grass, and animals singing in the distance, insects, frogs, he didn't know exactly. Above the barn he saw a light on in the room Estella had. There were steps cut into the hillside, and at the top, the door was partly open. But he couldn't tell if Jimmy was in there or not.

"I found two of my best fishing rods down at the dock this morning," Mack said at dinnertime the next day. "Now . . . " He paused, looked around the room at each of them. "I consider you my guests. And as guests, I hope you will make use of the equipment I have here. But anything you use I expect you to return in good condition to the spot you found it in. That's just my little rule. And it applies to everything—wading boots, fishing rods, life jackets, the jeep, the golf cart. Now the fishing rods probably weren't hurt by being outside, it wasn't raining, there wasn't even any dew, but when I saw them I had to ask myself who would be so careless with something that didn't belong to them."

Estella came in with a platter of roast lamb. Jimmy followed her with two bowls, one of mint jelly, one of gravy. They served Mack first, and when his plate was full he put his napkin on his lap and said, "Well, I'm sure you'll all respect my wishes. Even Nathan and Jimmy, right?"

"I'm sorry, sir," Nathan said. "I left them out. I just forgot."

"I left mine out, too," Jimmy said. "We won't do it again."

"Now that's impressive," Phyllis said to Mack.

"Hey, they're good kids," Mack said off-handedly. "Good kids."

Their mother and father were smiling. Everyone was smiling.

Molly, as though she were oblivious to what was going on, broke in with, "This is such tasty lamb, so tender."

Phyllis called, "Estella, you're getting compliments! Everyone loves your lamb!"

"Thank you," Estella called back. Jimmy appeared with a tureen of peas. She went to Mack first, but he waved her away, saying, "I might not be a healthy man, but peas are the one vitamin pill I don't take."

On Friday Nathan scored one hundred on Mademoiselle's test on nouns. That afternoon she started him on verbs by asking him which ones he wanted to learn. She handed him a fresh pencil from her pencil case, and he wrote down the first five that came to mind: to swim, to row, to walk, to dance, to worry.

"Does a boy who is your age like to dance?" Mademoiselle asked.

He said that he hated to dance.

"That is another one, to hate. Do you like to walk?"

"No," he told her, he hated it more than dancing.

"Then what do you like to do?" she asked.

He looked at her hard, angular chest, trussed up behind the shiny fabric of her blouse in a bra and slip and whatever other undergarments might be used by a middle-aged lady who needed to contain her blubber, and said that he liked to fish.

"Ah fish, all boys like to fish. Every time you fish, you think, *pêcher*. Tell me about the biggest fish you ever caught."

"I don't catch any."

"Ah, be patient. That is the answer to everything."

It was true. And patience was something that Nathan knew how to practice. At that moment, for instance, he was waiting for answers to several questions that had developed over the two weeks they'd been at Mack's place. The first was about Mack himself. What did he want with Nathan? The second had to do with Estella. What was she teaching Jimmy? The third was, when would disaster strike?

Nathan was fond of catastrophes: train wrecks, airplane crashes, hurricanes, tornadoes. One moment everything was its normal boring self, and the next moment the world was skewed to a weird angle and there was nothing familiar anywhere. Such amazing changes woke everybody up and gave them new energy. Because, as he saw it, everyone was drifting off to sleep, forgetting to pay attention. His mother was painting ponds in her studio all day long. His father was making vases. The dancers were twirling around on the lawn. According to Erik, they were stretching the limits of their bodies and experimenting with organic form. But when Nathan looked at them, he thought they were just out there trying to be children again.

Meanwhile, the world was drying up around them. The pond was evaporating, the dirt was crusting over, the leaves on everything were going brown. Grasshoppers were everywhere, clicking in and out of the dry grasses, and any fish that knew their business were hanging out down at the bottom of the pond, away from heat and fishermen and sunlight.

And Mack. Mack was taking him off to the forest every morning. Jimmy was spending more and more time up in the room over the barn with Estella. And sometimes she stayed with her in the kitchen after dinner, helping her to clean up. Nathan was on a campaign to be nice to *la sœur*, because if she disappeared completely, there would be no one out there at all.

That morning, after he'd dragged the water cart to every tree they'd put in over the last three days and given them such a long drink the big drum on the truck was halfway down, he'd gone back to wait until they were finished planting the new ones. He was also waiting for Mack, who had gone down to inspect the trees they'd put in last week.

When he came up to Nathan he was breathing heavily, and his face under the wide brim of the cowboy hat was as red as a piece of raw meat. "Hey Nathan, come here, there's something I want to show you."

Nathan followed him into an area of the forest where there were trees with thin shaggy trunks standing against the sky like prison bars. Mack squatted down and pushed some leaves away from a low green plant with small pink blossoms. "See this here. This is Herb Robert. Looks delicate, but Herb Robert can withstand a lot of tough weather before it gives up. A pretty little plant, isn't it? Might be one of those the Indians used for medicine. Who knows, might help with the very thing that ails you. Well, let's sit down next to Herb Robert." He plopped down to the ground heavily, took off his cowboy hat. "Hey, tell you what, I'd like to get you a present. Something you want, maybe something your parents won't buy."

Nathan looked up in surprise.

"Hell, that's nothing unusual. Your dad's an artist. He doesn't make a lot. But I'm a businessman and good or bad, business makes bucks. It's how the world works. And it's not fair, but the truth is I can afford to be generous. So maybe there's something that's too expensive or maybe . . . and here's the other part of it see . . . maybe there's something you really want, but your parents don't approve of, or you're scared to ask for. Something like that. I thought I'd see if you had any ideas."

"That's very nice of you, sir," Nathan said.

"A bike. Maybe you need a good bike."

"I don't particularly like bike riding," Nathan said.

"Well then. I know what. How 'bout I get you your own professional fishing rod? You'd like that."

"Well, sir, you have so many here already and I don't have a place to fish at home."

"Yeah, that's right. Well, . . . let's see. Your first suit. Custom fit by my tailor. Hey, that's something every young man needs. You got to look professional. A good suit gets you places. Opens doors."

"Well . . . " Nathan looked at the ground. "I guess I would feel bad that I was getting something and Jimmy wasn't."

Mack moved in closer. Now he was sitting on top of Herb Robert.

"You're crushing the flower," Nathan said.

"What? Oh, doesn't matter, it's just a plant, there's millions of them, right? Now . . . "

"It will heal what's ailing you," Nathan said quietly.

"Maybe so, but listen to me, I'll tell you what. I'll let you in on a little secret." He lowered his voice as though there were people around to hear them. "When I was your age, I thought about girls. Know what I mean? You want to see the right things. You're curious. How 'bout some pictures. Not just any old pictures. Explicit, revealing. Got me?"

Nathan didn't say anything, so Mack went on. "Naked. Now, I'm not talking women like your mother or your sister. I'm talking women raw, uncivilized, showing everything, and guys too. When I was your age, I had an uncle and he did things like that for me, things I would like to do for you. We could special order these, see, and they'd be here in two days and we'd find them a hiding place. No one else would know. And how about some candy bars and soda and chips, because I know your mother." He laughed. "Hey, with a mother like that a boy needs an uncle, so Mack's going to take care of you. Our little secret. Here, shake on it." He held out a beefy palm.

But Nathan put his hands in his pockets and said, "That's okay."

This time Mack extended his arm. "Here, give me a hand up."

But Nathan turned away, so Mack hoisted himself up, grunting and hanging onto the trunk of a tree. Walking out of the forest, he clapped a hand on Nathan's shoulder. It sat there like a piece of concrete until they got to the field, then Nathan ducked out from underneath it and ran off.

That afternoon he asked Jimmy if she wanted to go in the boat with him. She said okay, as long as he didn't fish, because she couldn't bear it if he cut up any more worms. There was still a pile of worm crud on the dock, and Nathan squatted down to see how they had decomposed. They weren't worms at all anymore, just old mud. So that's what happened when everything in you dried out; you were just a useless piece of nothing.

Jimmy pushed the boat into the water, and Nathan stepped into it from the dock, trying not to let it tip. But it did, and Jimmy had to grab onto the sides to keep from sliding out. "Don't ever do that again," she said. "You could have capsized us."

He apologized, then suggested they go under the willows, because he knew she liked the darkness underneath the hanging branches.

"No, let's stay out in the open."

He let her row, and she steered them out to the middle of the pond.

"Where's the underworld?" he asked.

She was hanging off the side of the boat, her fingers trailing in the water. "It's underneath us."

"What's in it?"

"All the spirits."

"What spirits?"

"All the spirits of the trees and the animals and the plants."

"So what are they down there for? I mean, what does it matter to us?"

"Lots," she said importantly.

"Come on, Jimmy, tell me."

"I don't know if Estella wants me to tell anybody else. It's sort of special. You can't just tell anybody."

"You can tell me. I'm your brother. And I know something about it too."

"What do you know?"

"I know about this plant called Herb Robert that can cure anything that's the matter with you and it grows in the shade and has a little pink blossom."

"Where does it grow?"

"Near where they've been planting the trees."

"Show me, okay?"

"I will if you tell me."

Jimmy sat up on the bench and hooked her hair behind her ears. In a different tone of voice she said, "See, how it works is they're down there to help us. What you have to do is dive down into the pond, all the way down, and then you have to find an animal to take you into the underworld."

"Yeah, and you drown in the process."

"I don't have to tell you any of this."

"I'm sorry. I really want to know, okay? I'm sorry."

"You don't dive down for real. You do it in your imagination. It's like playing a made-up game. And when you get to the under-world, you can ask a plant or a tree, whoever comes up to you, for help with your problem. We've been doing it a lot, Estella and me, up in her bedroom. Erik's drumming outside and the drum-ming helps us to stay focused."

"I have a problem."

"Okay, tell me, I'll go to the underworld tomorrow with Estella."

"I can't tell you."

"What's it about then?"

"It's about Mack."

"What happened?" Jimmy asked, looking worried.

"Nothing happened and nothing's going to happen." Suddenly, he didn't trust anything Jimmy was saying. "How do you know Estella's not playing a big joke on you? She's just a cook, she prob-ably never even finished high school."

"You don't have to be educated to know things. And she knows things because she grew up in Jamaica."

"She's from New York. I heard Mack talking about her. She lives in Brooklyn."

"Yeah, but she lived in Jamaica when she was a little girl."

"So, that doesn't mean anything."

"Well, you don't have to believe in it, Nathan. And if I do, that's my business." She picked the oars up and rowed them to-ward the swampy side of the pond. She didn't go far into it though; she stopped before the water got too shallow. Nathan could touch the cattails. He saw a bird's nest among them and craned his head to see if there were any eggs. He caught a spot of blue, startling against the dull colors of the rushes. It was a blue as pale as Mack's eyes.

"It hasn't rained in four weeks," Jimmy said.

"You think I don't know? I'm the one who has to water all those trees."

"Mack's worried."

"Who cares?"

"You might not like Mack, but you can care about the trees at least."

"They're his trees—why should I?"

"Estella's going to ask the spirits to help the trees."

"I'm sure she is."

"She's going to ask them to bring rain."

"Rain happens when the right atmospheric conditions are present. And when they're present, it will rain. And it won't if they're not there."

"Do you know something? You're ignoring something very obvious. What people think affects the world. What they want affects the world. What they ask for . . . if they ask for it with respect, it will happen."

"Sure. I want a car and a car's going to appear."

"You have to ask for it with respect, and it has to be a natural thing like rain."

"So what if there isn't a natural thing that I want? I'm not ever going to get anything?"

Jimmy ignored the question. "I want rain. Estella wants rain. The trees want rain. It's going to rain."

He looked at her with hatred.

"Not for Mack," she added. "I want rain for the trees."

That afternoon when Mademoiselle came, she asked him to write down fifteen verbs as quickly as possible As he did it, she went to the sink and filled two glasses with water. She put one in front of him and sat down across from him and drank hers.

"Quickly, quickly, we have much to do."

He pushed the paper across to her. She looked at his words and then wrote the French beside the English. When she was done, the list looked like this:

to swim—*nager*
to follow—*suivre*
to suspect—*soupçonner*
to laugh—*rire*
to cry—*pleurer*
to dive—*plonger*
to find—*trouver*
to worry—*s'inquiéter*
to row—*ramer*
to watch—*regarder*
to fear—*craindre*
to fall—*tomber*
to give up—*abandonner*
to refuse—*refuser*
to kick—*donner des coups de pied*

"This is just a little test I do with my students. *Une évaluation psychologique.* Okay?" She put a check beside suspect, cry, worry, fear, fall, give up, refuse, kick. "Eight negatives. Seven positives. You are borderline, Nathan. That is, there is much that is on your mind, and it threatens to overtake your happiness, but it hasn't yet. I suggest to you to have more fun. It will help with the worry, the suspicion, the fear. Right? And you mustn't feel bad about it. Everyone worries, everyone suspects, everyone is afraid. It is human nature. Remove those feelings to the side and have fun. If it is French you are worried about, you are a superior student. Just keep studying your words and you'll be fine. Next time, if you have learned all of the verbs, I will bring you a reward. That is something you can look forward to, yes?"

The screen door opened and his father walked in. His pants were covered with clay, and he tracked clay across the floor. "Hi Nathan! *Bonjour . . .* "

Nathan could tell that *le père* had intended to say the French teacher's name but then discovered that he no longer remembered what it was.

"If you'll excuse me, I'm just going to make myself a sandwich, and then I'll be out of your way."

Nathan hoped his father wouldn't be too obvious about the kind of sandwich he was making. Peanut butter and banana would strike a French woman as being pretty weird. Add to it his father's ragged clothes and his goofy good humor. But Mademoiselle wasn't paying attention. She was pronouncing each word on the list and pausing for him to repeat it after her. *Pleurer. Plonger. Nager. Ramer.* He noticed that what Mademoiselle called his positive verbs had to do with water.

Jimmy played "Für Elise" during cocktails. Each evening when she sat down at the piano he would think, "Not again!" But then the song would start, and no matter how aloof he tried to be, the music pulled him in. It was so melodious, so seductive, so full of all his hidden feelings, he had to listen. The piece was a perfect balance of logic and emotion. Maybe all music was that way. Well, he knew one thing for sure. Dance was only emotion. Painting was only emotion. That's why they weren't pure art like music.

People had moved onto the patio because it was so hot. Nathan went outside, too. He stood against the cool wall of the house close to the window so he could continue to listen. No one else paid any attention. *La mère*, sitting across from him, was laughing loudly. She wore a pink dress with a ruffled neckline, and her bare arms, freckled from the sun, were pretty. Molly was laughing, too. Her blouse was unbuttoned so far down he could see her bosom looking at him straight on. Natalie was standing in a corner talking in an animated way with Erik. She had very white skin and dark hair, and there was something quick and silvery about her, she flashed in and out. Nathan tried to imagine her having sex with Erik. He pictured a billowing, a glistening, a rising of bodies that happened simultaneously, as though they were both listening to the same melody in their heads. It would get louder, they would rise higher and higher, and then finally it would burst, just as it did now on the piano. The piece ended, there was a pause, and then a little bit later, the opening measures sounded again. Molly put down her drink, and saying "Excuse me," went into the house. Nathan pulled himself away from the wall and followed her. What if she knew he was following her and had ducked into an empty bedroom to wait for him, and when he came after, she closed the door and turned to face him, her blouse open all the way down? Nipples was a subject he hardly dared to think about.

She stopped at the olives, took some, and then went into the living room. He stayed back in the shadows, but at a spot where he could see her waving her arms to get Jimmy's attention. But Jimmy was in the song. Her eyes were closed, her body was swaying. "Jimmy!"

The bitch broke the trance. Jimmy looked up, startled. "Excuse me?"

"Don't you know any other songs? I mean, is this the only one you can play?"

"I like this one."

Molly's nipples would be large; he would eat them.

"Well, why don't you give us all a break and play something else for a while."

Jimmy looked at her uncomprehendingly. Then she started the song where she had stopped, staring at Molly until she turned around and left.

By that time, Nathan was sitting on the couch. "Hi!" he said in a friendly way.

She gave him an annoyed look. Then she took the olive pits out of her mouth and put them in the ashtray.

"I bet you don't know what I am."

"No, I guess not."

Nathan looked at her smugly, daring himself to go on. "I'm a superior student. Would you be my teacher?"

Molly went out, letting the screen door slam behind her.

Because it was so hot, Estella served a light meal. There were salads and thinly sliced bread and cold cuts. Jimmy brought everything out to the sideboard in the dining room, and everyone helped themselves. Phyllis said, "Mack, why should we sit in here? We'll be much cooler if we eat outside."

"There's only two tables, Phyllis. It won't be very comfortable."

"The kids can put their plates on their laps, can't they? Do you want to do that, Nathan?"

"Sure."

"Jimmy?"

"Jimmy's in the kitchen with Estella."

"Oh right, I forgot."

"I'm ready," Erik said suddenly, and stood up with his napkin and plate. Everyone else followed him outside.

The patio looked out over the lawn that tumbled down to the willows and the pond. Nathan pulled his chair to the edge of the patio and looked at the view. Behind him, he heard *la mère* say to Mack and Phyllis, "You need some swans on that pond and some peacocks strutting around with their tails open."

"Then you've got bird poop," Mack said.

"Sweetie, Judy wasn't being serious. She was just talking about fantasy. No one wants you to actually go out and do it. Everyone's very happy with just the way things are."

"Well, there is one thing," Judy said.

"What is it? Tell me, you know I'm always looking for suggestions." That was Phyllis.

"Next summer, if you do this again, how about inviting a couple of musicians and a writer or two?"

"Terrific idea! A regular artist colony. Right here in West Redding, Connecticut. The only problem is the musicians. We'd have to build them studios in the woods, otherwise they'd disturb the writers."

"And then at the end of the summer," his mother went on, "everyone could do a grand collaboration."

"A piece of cacophonous nonsense," his father added.

"Nonsense it might be," *la mère* agreed, "but it would be fun."

Nathan remembered Mademoiselle's advice to have more fun. The word was meaningless. It was one of those trick words, like "happy." If you thought about fun or happiness, it meant that you weren't feeling the real thing. For it to be the real thing, you had to be unaware of it. He looked down at the pond and realized there was movement at the end of the dock. Was it Natalie and Erik? But it couldn't be, they were sitting at a table with Molly.

Now there was a large white bird gliding over the water. "Mom!" he called.

But she was laughing at something Phyllis had said. Her cheeks were the same color as her dress, and by the time she had finished the bird was gone. He could see who was down there now. It was Jimmy with someone in a chair next to her, whom he assumed was Estella. He wondered if they'd seen the bird too. For a moment, he thought about running down there to ask, but then he noticed their heads were almost touching and they seemed to be deeply involved in whatever they were doing.

On most nights, it started to cool down by nine o'clock. But that evening, it seemed to get hotter. Phyllis brought out candles on footed candlesticks and set them around the patio. There were two games of cards going. *Le père* pulled a chair up next to Nathan. "I was so embarrassed today. I couldn't remember your French teacher's name. Do you think she noticed? What is it any-way?"

"Mademoiselle Bruneau."

"Bruneau. Well, I'll try to get it right next time."

"It's okay, I don't think she noticed."

"So how's it going?"

"Fine."

"Do things seem familiar? Is she covering the same sorts of things you got in school?"

"Oh, much more."

"And are you paying attention and studying?"

"Yes."

"I hope so, because we're paying her a good salary. I'll tell you something, this French isn't coming to you cheap."

"If I went to summer school back home it would be free."

"Summer school? Are you still wishing you were going to summer school? Do you know how hot it is in Philadelphia right now? You think this is bad. And you can swim here and fish and boat, and you and your sister are free to do whatever you want all day long. It seems to me you're about the luckiest kid in the world."

"I know, Dad."

But that didn't satisfy his father, because he went on. "When I think back to the summers I spent in Cleveland when I was your age, living in an apartment, no place to swim . . . You're in paradise thanks to Mack and Phyllis. You know that?"

"Yes, Dad."

The moon came up over the willows. The bull frogs croaked down at the pond, and all around them in the grass, insects sang.

"Last one in's a rotten egg!" Erik called. He ran across the patio, Natalie behind him.

A few moments later there were splashes in the water. "Hey, it's nice!" Natalie called.

"Are they going skinny-dipping?" Molly asked the people on the terrace.

Nathan ran down the lawn in his bare feet. The pond was a bowl of moonlight. The frogs had gone silent, and he could hear Natalie call, "Over here, I'm over here!" Nathan stepped onto the dock and slipped out of his clothes. He was careful to leave them in a pile separate from the others, so he'd be able to find them again. "No silly, over here!" The air felt good on the tender parts of his body. Suddenly there was a lot of splashing. Laughter. He wondered if Jimmy was in the pond too, and then realized, of course she was. "Watch out everybody," he called, "I'm diving in!"

The superior student's pubescent body knifed through the moon, scattering it into fragments. "Is that you, Nathan?" Jimmy asked. She swam over to him, her disembodied face floating on the surface of the water.

"Did you see that bird swooping over the pond?" he asked her.

"You saw it too?"

"Yeah, it was amazing."

"Not so loud," Jimmy whispered. Her eyes looked enormous. He plinked a little water in her direction and in a low voice said, "What was it?"

"Just Estella. See . . . " Jimmy pointed up at the lawn, and Nathan saw the same great white form crossing it at the top. "It's her uniform, it glows."

"But it looked like she was out in the middle of the water."

"It looked like it because you were seeing it with your imagi-

nation. That's the best way to see everything." Without any warning, she flipped back and floated away from him.

"Hey!" he called after her. There were another three splashes
into the pond. He could feel people moving toward him. He
swam away quickly, because he hated them all and the only one
he wanted to be with was Jimmy. "Jimmy!" he whispered.

"Over here," she said from the direction of the willows.

"Wait for me!" he cried.

"I'll wait, but hurry."

Soundlessly, he stroked across the water and got away.
"Jimmy?"

"Come in closer," she whispered, "but you have to be very
quiet."

He saw her white arm on top of the water and swam toward
it. She reached out and pulled him in. Then he saw her face, her
blue lips, her black eyes, strings of hair. "If we stay very still, the
frogs'll start singing again. But we have to be very still."

"Those guys out there are making a racket."

She put her finger to her lips. "Shh! They'll go away soon, and
the frogs will think we went with them. Just be quiet."

His penis was so shriveled from the cold water it was no bigger than his pinkie. He was a nothing, worse than a nothing, a
clump of worm crud. Jimmy looked at him steadily. He trusted
her more than he trusted anyone else in the world. So he stayed
there, treading water beside her. Their bodies hung in the pond,
just outside the branches of the willows, and after a while the
voices at the other end went away. He heard laughter on the
lawn. "You're wearing my shirt!" someone cried. After that, it was
quiet. Sometime later, he wondered if *le père* and *la mère* were

back at the cottage, and if they had noticed their children were gone. Maybe they'd come searching with flashlights. They'd make so much noise the frogs would never start singing again. He was about to suggest to Jimmy that they give up. But then he heard a croak. And then another one. Soon there was croaking all around them, and then there were strumming and trilling sounds. All the different kinds of frogs were singing into the night. The amphibian population was arranged around the edges of a pond they had assumed was empty, and he and Jimmy were suspended together in the middle of it, listening.

Later, much later, when even the moon was covered over by a cloud, they climbed back onto the dock. They put on whatever clothes they could find and didn't even try to look for their shoes, but started up the lawn barefoot. When they reached the big house the candles were still burning on the patio, and there were voices, hardly audible against the sounds of the night. Nathan heard Mack's gravelly laugh. He knew that in another step they'd throw out shadows, so he grabbed Jimmy by the wrist and pulled her away. They started to laugh when they got to the barn. Nathan led Jimmy out to the grassy circle inside the curve of the driveway, and they both lay down inside it.

"I hate Mack," Nathan said.

"Why?"

"He wants to buy me magazines." He knew that wouldn't make any sense to Jimmy, so he added, "So I can look at naked girls."

Jimmy laughed. "What's so bad about that?"

"He's creepy."

"He's nice to me."

"That's because he doesn't want to have sex with you."

Jimmy was quiet. He didn't know if she understood how a man could have sex with a boy, but it didn't matter. The thing was said, and he felt better.

"I went to the underworld. I talked to the willow tree, and a frog was my messenger."

"How'd you do that?"

"In my imagination."

"But Jimmy, maybe it's all made up then."

He could tell he'd disappointed her, because she said in a defensive tone, "It is and it isn't. It just has to do with what you want to believe."

"So what did you say to them?"

"That I had a brother and he needed protection."

"You did? But how will they be able to find me?"

"They'll be able to, don't worry."

"But how? Maybe they'll think it's Erik."

"They'll know, Nathan. I told them who you are. They'll find you."

That night there was drumming in his sleep. Erik was just outside the window, calling to him with his drum. Though Nathan wanted to keep sleeping, the sound was hypnotic, and he was soon climbing out of the window to join him. Natalie, Molly, and Jimmy made a circle around him, reaching for his hand, and with Erik at the lead, they snaked in and out of the trees.

Nathan wasn't thinking about anything; he was just moving to the sounds, noticing every so often how loose and relaxed he felt. Then he was with Jimmy, and they were diving off the dock into the pond. He opened his eyes underwater and followed his sister's naked body down into the grass at the bottom. An oak tree grew down there. Jimmy said, "Hello, oak tree. I'd like to come to the underworld. Would you send me an escort?" A red fox ran up, and Jimmy got onto its back and disappeared. Nathan stayed by the tree. After a while it seemed apparent that an escort wasn't going to come for him. Finally the tree broke the silence, and in a voice that matched his father's, it said, "Don't you know, son, nothing comes without the asking."

Nathan looked into the watery darkness and asked, "Please, can you send me an escort?"

"You can ask," the tree replied, "but asking only works if it's something you truly want."

The next morning the sky was green. At first the sun shone weakly, but then it was covered over by white clouds. The air was very humid. As his parents and the dancers dug holes for the trees, the shovels clanked against the rocks loudly. Nathan was pulling the water cart along the row of already planted trees, giving each one a good drink. The tiny leaves were the same green as the sky. They were starting to yellow, particularly on the trees that had been planted earlier in the summer, so Nathan gave those the most water. He squatted down and nestled the hose right in the roots. "There," he said, "you'll like that. That's just what you want. Isn't that good? Yes, that's just what you've been missing." No one was around, and after he situated the hose, he counted to three hundred, and then moved it to the next tree. The water spilled over his sneakers, made pools of dirt with leaves and blossoms floating on top. Something flickered. It was white and out of place. Mack's white shirt, above it the red meat of his jowls.

"Who're you talking to, Nathan?"

"Nobody."

"But I just heard you say something. Who were you talking to, boy?"

"Myself."

Mack chucked him on the shoulder. "Hey! Have I got something for you!" He reached into a paper bag and pulled out a thin, glossy magazine.

"No thank you."

Water was carrying away the peat moss that had been laid around the base of the tree.

"Here she is." Mack flung the magazine open, and there on the ground was Molly, unbuttoned and bare. He saw the nipples and the mysterious place he had always wondered about, and as he looked at her, he noticed the changes inside of him.

"Touch her, Nathan. Go ahead." Mack guided his fingers to the very spot he had been looking at. He knew he was touching a picture, a stupid picture, so it wasn't a big deal. But still he wanted to. He wanted to feel it with his whole body, he wanted to pull his pants off and roll around on top of it. He wanted to put the picture into his mouth and eat her. He didn't notice that the hose was running over his leg. But he smelled something.

Mack's tongue was moving around in his ear, and his hand was on Nathan's thigh, but what he smelled was the pungent scent of the earth as the water moistened it. Mack's hand was in his crotch, making him so hard he was afraid he was going to explode. Then Mack started to unzip his pants, but the zipper didn't move. Mack tried again. Nathan saw the beefy fingers fumbling at his hips, and right then, just as the man finally got the zipper to go down, he felt himself ejaculate. He slapped the hands away and jumped up. But the hose caught on his foot and flipped up into Mack's lap. Mack cursed as the water gurgled over his clothes, but Nathan didn't hear anything, he was streaking through the woods, running like a scared child. He ran past the planters, past the truck, and then ducked back into the woods and made his way down the hillside. When he reached the cottage, the first thing he did was run into the bathroom. He ripped off his clothes and stood in the shower in his underwear, letting the water run as hot as he could stand. Then he peeled the sticky drawers off his body and leaving the shower running, stuffed them in the trashcan under the kitchen sink. He ran back through his wet footprints, got back into the shower, and soaped and shampooed vigorously.

By the time Mademoiselle arrived he was dressed. The floor was wiped up and the trash can under the sink was empty, because he'd dumped the entire contents into the incinerator.

"Did you study your verbs, Nathan?"

He gave her the list and was able to pronounce each correctly.

"*Très bien!* Now I will give you my reward!"

He had forgotten about the reward, and when she took out a paperback book written in French with a title he didn't understand, he said, "*Merci, Mademoiselle.*"

"We will start reading this soon, once you've finished your sentences. What's it called? Can you tell me?"

"*Le Chien d'Anton.*"

"And what does that mean? Eh? Do you know?" When he didn't respond, she said, "Well, we haven't done the animals, so I will tell you. The dog of Anton. Anton's dog. It is a story about a lost dog and how a boy who doesn't have a mother finds him. It is a very sweet story. I give it to all of my students. Now, you know nouns, you know verbs, next we will put them together with connecting words and make sentences. Once you see how to make a sentence, we can really talk to one another."

She wrote "I am" and then left a blank. "Very quickly, I want you to write as many words as you can think of to finish this. For instance, I am tired could be one." She pushed the paper over to him. She had written "tired" in the blank.

He just looked at it stupidly.

"This is so easy, so *facile*, Nathan. Quickly do it, five or six more words."

So he wrote:

I am lost.
I am hot.
I am curious.
I am lumpy.
I am stretched.

"Okay." She looked at the list of words but didn't say anything, only printed the French above the English. "Now I am is, *je suis*. So each of these sentences begins with *je suis*. Some of these don't make too much sense, but if they are the words you want, okay. For instance, what does I am lumpy mean? Eh? I am stretched? It doesn't make sense. So I have given you what I think you may mean. Okay, now let's think of some ordinary sentences that begin with *je suis*.

Je suis affamé.
Je suis beau.
Je suis un homme."

By the time Mademoiselle was ready to leave, the sky had darkened. "It looks like rain," she said when Nathan walked her to the Citroën.

The novel sat on the kitchen table. He carried it into his room and hid it under his underwear in the top dresser drawer.

When he went outside again, the sky was the color of lead. Wind shook the tops of the birches, blew the leaves to their undersides. He had to push into the wind as he walked down the road. He wanted to find Jimmy, but he didn't want to risk running into Mack. The rain started when he got to the pond. No Jimmy. He slammed through the bathhouse, but they never went there, and he knew she wouldn't be there now. He ran back up the lawn and swung behind the main house to the barn. It was pouring steadily, water pulsing out of the gutters, flooding the driveway. The tempo increased. A curtain of water hiding the world. He ran up the steps at the side of the barn and pounded on Estella's door at the top. Water spilled off the roof onto his head. Lightning tore across the sky, then, over the house, a clash of thunder. He tried the knob, because he didn't think anyone could hear him in that racket, and the door opened. The room was as sparsely furnished as a jail cell, with a trunk and a single bed with a blanket on it. No rug, no pictures, no bedspread. Another reason to hate Mack and Phyllis.

Nathan ran through the downpour, over to the main house, and peered into the kitchen window. Estella was kneading dough on the counter, but Jimmy wasn't there. He was about to tap the glass to get her attention when Mack walked into the kitchen, opened the refrigerator, and took out a bottle of beer. Estella turned to say something to him, and Mack laughed.

Nathan started to head back to the cottage. His shoes were so wet they were spongy. Water slid down his eyes, spilled off his hair and into the neck of his shirt. There was no use in hurrying, he was completely soaked. He saw a light on in his mother's cottage. Find refuge there? He would leak buckets of water onto her floor.

The wind tossed the tops of the trees, ripped across the lawn. He ran through the grass. It was at that moment that lightning split the sky in half and the same winged creature he had seen on the pond swooped over the mowed area and fell down. He started to run toward it, but his sneakers flopped off, and without stopping he ran out of them and through the pools of water. Jimmy was lying on the ground, her clothes stuck onto her skin. Was she dead? Panicking, he called her name. But it was too noisy, his voice was lost in roaring air. He knelt over her, and her face burst into a smile.

"I told them we needed rain. And it's raining. Isn't that amazing?"

"Yeah," he said, "but it's lightning and you're out in the open."

"You're out in the open too, and you're higher than me. And I have rubber soles on my sneakers, and you don't even have your sneakers on. You'd better lie down really flat. Come on, get rained on."

So he lay down next to her, and water pounded on his body till he turned flat and muddy. He wasn't even a boy anymore. Next to him, Jimmy wasn't even a girl. They were rivers of water. They were grass, they were ground, they were sky.

Salt

She had lived in the best cities of the United States and Europe, in the best times, but at age fifty-eight, she'd ended up near a small college town in western New York State that was so rural there were more coyote than people. And so poor that between the two, the coyote were the ones more gainfully employed. Their job was to keep the deer population in check. They couldn't touch the bear or the occasional cougar, and they managed the deer by killing the fawns.

The people were scattered in valley pockets and across the hills; they were hunters and farmers, and watching the deer population decrease, they cursed the DEC, which they claimed had imported the coyote into the county. But it was the rocks, the clay soil, the endless precipitation that were the real reasons for their bitterness. Nature never eased up. On that loamy hard-pan, conditions were propitious for the mammals who grazed. Which meant that the tenders of gardens and dwellers in houses saw little payback for all their hard work.

And yet, beginning with the bursts of the Juneberry blossoms on the hillsides in May, when the three months of summer stretched their gaudy seductions before them, even these prag-matists, these scorners of extravagance, purchased flowers: petu-nias, pansies, marigolds. She sold truckloads of annuals out of the shack she rented by the hardware store, and the income from the three months she was in operation was just enough to keep her going for the rest of the year. She also sold vegetable plants, herbs, and a small selection of perennials. But what she sold best, and was herself most hungry for when the earth fi-nally greened up after the long winter and the new shiny leaves on trees and bushes rippled in the milky winds, was color, the massive and dependable color of annuals solid packed into a bed in the backyard, or overflowing from a pot on the patio. It was her way of keeping some of nature's abundance for herself, mim-icking the insouciance of the vines, brambles, reeds, plants, grasses that fructified even on the most inhospitable slopes.

She was not a native. And to survive the lifestyle she'd cho-sen, she held onto small esoteric, idiosyncratic reminders of the other places she'd been, the other ways of living. *Fructify* was one of those, a word imported from better times. When Mario Cuomo was the governor of New York State, he'd used it in a con-versation with the former senator Patrick Moynihan. She'd been driving somewhere, too stoned to follow the context, when the word blazed out of the radio. She was surprised a politician had the courage to use it. But that was a long time ago, when the public would tolerate unusual language. Even she, Claudia Jane Hanley, living more, or mostly less, productively in the eastern part of the state, had looked it up in the dictionary when she got home. Fructify: to bear fruit.

This summer everything had greened up, but the fructifying was not happening as it should. On Memorial Day weekend, people visited her shop, and in gardens all over the county her flower and vegetable plants waited in neat rows, but the rains never came. The whole month of June was dry like a desert. Then July arrived, and nothing changed. She could count on one hand the rainy days in that two-month period. Normally, there was so much precipitation the fructifying happened in a bold and reckless manner. Wildflowers carpeted the fields, waxy new growth dressed the evergreens. Now the plants in the garden were stunted, the fields had hardly any blossoms. The ancient sugar maple by the house, its massive trunk growing straight up by the corner of the porch and its first limbs casting an umbrella of shade over the roof, looked dusty. The other day, on two separate dirt roads, a great blue heron had stepped out in front of her car, its big, mud-accustomed feet lifting up and coming down uncertainly on the hard-packed surface. This summer there wasn't any mud for him, there weren't any shallow pools, and the streams were mostly dried up.

Standing by the back door, looking out at a colorless meadow (where were the bright cheeks of birdsfoot trefoil?), Claudia tasted the hot air and thought to herself, *That man knows what he's talking about.* The man she was referring to was not her most recent husband (last seen in 2001), or the boyfriend who had sped away on his motorcycle the day she opened the garden shop and most needed his help (two years ago, 2005), but Mr. Birdsall on the opposite hill, who, in April, had bent down and picked up a clod of dirt which he crumbled into his thick, calloused palm. He held a piece between his blunt-ended fingers and placed it in his mouth, chewing silently, looking not at her but at the next hill, where the evening sun simmered at the tree line. "It's gonna be a dry summer," he pronounced. "Best hope you sell your flowers early and fast. Come Independence Day, streams gonna be dead and wells dried up." He pushed his cap forward, toed the earth with a cracked leather boot, and said, "Yup. My grandpa. Lived to be ninety-seven. Never left the county but once. He could taste the wind and tell you a hundred things. Some summers he called sweet. Others he called salt. This one'll be salt. Rain's gonna be real thin."

It was now the middle of July. Her well was deep, but she'd heard of others who'd had problems. Claudia glanced over to the road, across the hill, her eyes sweeping the fields and streams and woodlands she paid taxes on, her glance moving back to the road which cut through in an S curve, and at that very moment a long forgotten sound filled her ears, and then a mirage topped the rise and came slowly around the bend to downshift, noisily, into her driveway. Then the ping-pong sound of simple mechanics stopped, a door opened in a high rectangular box sitting on small wheels, and a tall woman stepped down. It was an ancient VW bus, newly painted white on the top, yellow on the bottom, with the signature white cravat in the front and the fence-like bumpers. The yellow matched the woman's hair, the tips of which dangled in the ruts of the driveway as she bent over, her fingertips grazing her toes, and bounced for a while. Then she stood up, the hair flew back, and she twisted her long slender torso one way and then another, hands on her hips.

Claudia stood where she was, because at fifty-eight, she felt she'd earned the right to stay still a little longer and let things unfold. And sure enough, the blonde started doing jumping jacks while the passenger door opened and one thick pale ankle descended. From the pudgy toes and rubber sandal dangling off them, Claudia knew this was not another obsessive exerciser but her daughter Ingrid. That meant the other one was Sarah or Sandy, the friend she was traveling with. They would be stopping for a day or two so that Ingrid could get her stuff, and then they were driving to California, where the friend and Ingrid had transferred for their junior year.

Ingrid was exactly the female version of her father, Claudia's first husband, a curly-headed, sincere person who fructified somewhere on the West Coast, where he not only supplied the possibility for in-state tuition but ran an adult day care center, a harmless occupation he was probably good at.

Three things happened next, in this order: Sarah or Sandy finished up with knee bends, Ingrid turned around to pull an olive-colored canvas bag out of the front seat, and Claudia stepped off the back porch and walked down the driveway.

"There you are! Oh it's so good to see you! It's so open here! What a wonderful view. And you can see in all directions!" Ingrid cried, hand over her eyes, looking from the house to the pond, to the barn, to the automobile and farm-implement graveyard east of the barn, to the greenhouse coming off it to the south. When she was finished, she threw her arms around her mother's neck

and gripped her in an enthusiastic embrace that Claudia duti-
fully returned and then stepped away from so she could study
her only child. It had been more than a year. Ingrid had grown
pale and very feminine, her hair in long dark ringlets and her big
innocent eyes protected, since she was eight years old, by glasses
that magnified their guileless stare.

"Mommy, mommy, mommy!" Ingrid cried and threw her arms
around her again. In this second embrace, the plump cushioned
body Claudia had given birth to melted away some of her own
body's brittleness. Ingrid was like the long absent rain on hard
packed soil, and her mother, standing on the brown hilltop
she'd made her home, realized she was thirsty.

That was when Sarah or Sandy—no it was an unusual name,
Sula then—came over.

"Sash, this is my mother, Claudia."

The girl was a goddess. Claudia could see tiny blond hairs,
backlit by the sun, skimming her arms and legs. She towered
like an Olympian on the driveway, but her face had the same
guileless expression. How did these women manage to reach the
age of twenty-one and not have any disappointments? Were their
relationships so wholesome, so honest that there wasn't even a
drop of something held back in reserve? Apparently not. The S
girl's whole face turned toward her, beaming. Like a sun, as
though she needed more of that. Claudia crossed her arms over
her shrunken, loosely drooping breasts. She said, "Excuse me, I
didn't quite get your name?"

A hand came out, she was offering it for a shake, and Claudia
heard her say, "Sasha Wren."

"Ren? How do you spell that?" It would be R-E-N or possibly

R-E-N-N or maybe even R-E-H-N. So when she said W-R-E-N, Claudia felt herself blanch as much as a woman could who worked outdoors most of the day.

"Sasha Wren?" she asked, even though she knew very well that was what the girl had said. But it couldn't be. "Is Arthur Wren your father?" And as soon as that name was out of her mouth, the empty years collapsed and she was young again, her breasts were full and eager, and VW buses like that were everywhere. A fire was glowing in the darkness, and Arthur had just told her he'd gone into town to get a vasectomy. Casually, like it was a bottle of Jim Beam he was talking about, and in that deeply melodious voice thickened by the cigarettes they both smoked. "I have no desire to contribute to the continuation of the human species." It was a sentiment she shared, but she was on the pill, that altogether revolutionary and liberating tab of chemical hormones she swallowed every morning. A vasectomy was bold and reckless. It was truly saying no thanks to the future. She respected him for such a brave move, and when they had sex, she discovered that it had changed him. He was beyond simple biological needs. He was smart and adult. Sublime . . . even, she was to think later, mythological. There were no grunts or adjustments. It was just one smooth and continuous movement, the ballet of a strange and beautiful many-limbed creature.

Of course, those were the days before AIDS, when mostly what a girl had to worry about was bad drugs and crabs. And she'd certainly had both of those. But Arthur Wren, where was he, who had he become?

"He's my uncle," Sasha was saying. "My father's twin brother. I see him all the time."

"Your father?" A name came back: Basker Wren. He was the

reason Arthur had left. He called his brother Basket Case. Basket Case was throwing tantrums because Arthur had been gone so long and Basker was tired of being the only one to care for the estate and the parents and the horses. They had some big horse deal and lots of money. The facts of his life in Northern California, growing grapes, breeding quarter horses, training draft horses, and in general doing high-class things like that, cowed a girl who had spent her childhood in a rowhouse on Smick Street in Philadelphia. It hadn't occurred to her that he would leave his woman for a lifestyle and a brother. But he had. And on the rebound from that sad, sorry episode she'd met Ingrid's father and given in to those mere biological drives by forgetting to take her little plastic pill case on a camping trip.

"Well, come in!" Claudia said, walking toward the house Ingrid was about to see for the first time. Though it was hardly different from a dozen other damaged, rural homesteads she'd rented over the years, this was the first one she'd owned, and she was suddenly embarrassed to remember the ripped screen on the front door, the tattered carpet in the hallway. "You'll have to give Arthur my regards. It was a long time ago, but we were major people in each other's lives."

They walked under the long, graceful branches of the tree and through the door, across the carpet (yes, it was as horrible as she thought) back into the dark, paneled kitchen, where they sat at the table and she took out ice-cold beers.

The day unwound, and as one thing led to another thing and Ingrid exclaimed over Claudia's accomplishments ("It's such a big garden, Mom," "What an ingenious compost system," and at the greenhouse, "You replaced that whole wall of glass?"), everyone quickly relaxed and became pals. The pond was down two feet, the water too murky for swimming, so they sprayed each other with the hose, watered the garden, and walked on her path through the woods. The girls even helped her clean out the chicken house, moving wheelbarrows of precious manure-laden straw to the garden, where row upon row of thirsty plants stretched their spindly necks to the sky.

"This is our day of fun," Ingrid announced, sweating profusely as she shoveled chicken shit onto the wheelbarrow. "Tomorrow we'll start to pack."

Sasha had driven all the way from Massachusetts, so after dinner she excused herself and went to bed. Ingrid and her mother were back in the kitchen by then. The drying rack was heaped with clean dishes, because the dishwasher was broken; it had been since she bought the place. They had put the left-overs away and were wiping the stove and counter when evening came into the room, softening everything, making Ingrid talkative. "Arthur's the one who started the organic vineyard. He works outside all day like you do. Except he does it all year long, cause it's California. He's really nice; he took me and Sasha riding." She blushed. Speaking about her mother's former lover embarrassed her.

But Claudia didn't flinch. She stilled her eyes, forced herself to consider her bare brown hilltop from the point of view of a man who had miles of vineyard. "Beer?" she asked. But Ingrid wanted herbal tea. She searched the cupboards till she found some ancient tea bags in the back behind the bottle of vinegar.

Claudia returned the beer to the fridge. She'd been drinking too much anyway, she knew that.

"I'm sure I told you about him," Claudia said, wondering if this whole thing were a set up and the girls had some elaborate and totally ridiculous plan to get the two of them back together. Because maybe Arthur had felt the same surge of joy when he'd heard Ingrid's name. Except he wouldn't have recognized it. Ingrid had her father's name. But maybe he'd been searching for her all of these years; maybe he'd heard about that marriage.

No, it didn't matter. If they were to meet, she would ignore the long, limber body that used to wind itself around her so that she felt cared for and loved even in her extremities, and say to the older, but still beautiful face, *Forget it. It took me my whole life to get over you. You think I want to go through that again?* Then she'd breathe in the wonderful purifying air of a woman's cherished disappointments and tell him the past was past. They were done.

"I don't think so," Ingrid said, "or if you did, I don't remember."

Of course, maybe this denial was part of their plan. "Sasha looks like him. The same tall, sinewy, long-legged . . . "

"He's really handsome," Ingrid supplied.

"Oh my god, you should have seen him back then. I was in love with that man. This was Him, I thought." She could hear the phlegm in her voice, the years of smoking.

"So what happened?" Ingrid asked, sipping her tea and looking at her mother innocently.

But Claudia couldn't speak. Bitterness washed over her, closing her throat. Who *was* this girl of her loins? What charmed world did *she* live in? She looked at the yellowed counter with its cuts and gouges a text from someone's Friday night argument, witness of someone else's violent relationship, which she was too poor to get rid of. "What do you *think* happened?" she said, sliding the drawer on the table open, slipping a cigarette out of the pack, grabbing her lighter.

"Mom, please."

How could Ingrid's voice still be so childlike? She didn't live in her plush, rounded body; she didn't understand its needs.

"I thought you stopped."

"I guess so," Claudia said, putting the lighter down and reaching for a tab of Nicorette, also in that drawer, which she popped onto her tongue and sucked without enthusiasm.

"You really want to be hooked up to oxygen?"

"Not really," she said, deciding that when and if she had more X-rays of her lungs she would never again reveal the results to her daughter.

"Not *really*?" Ingrid repeated, her dark round magnified eyes settling their indelible stare on Claudia's face. "Not *really*?" This time she said it more softly. "When you already have the beginnings of emphysema and the doctor said if you stopped smoking now the spots would go away? You really want to be on oxygen in another year?"

"Really. Yes, really, that would be a very nice thing. Because we're fucked, Ingrid. Did you see the garden? In all my years of gardening I've never had a garden like that. And it's not because I didn't prepare the soil. I tilled in truckloads of manure, straw, sand. I made that earth good. But there's no rain. The yellow squash? Did you see it? It's like a dwarf, twelve inches high, but it's already making fruit. It's like a pregnant eight-year-old." She bit down on the gum, flipped it around in her mouth. Then she said, "June twenty-second, that was when I had to close the shop. Three weeks early. Two hundred plants rotting over there in the compost. All of that money, that effort. But what was I supposed to do? No one was buying."

She couldn't look at Ingrid's face; it was the counter with its mysterious gouges that allowed her to continue. "People around here are not set up to water their gardens. Especially when they're worried about their wells. And you know what they say. It's not just that it's a weird summer. It's the changing of the climate, the melting of the Arctic ice, the beginning of the end of the whole goddamned . . . " Anger swirled in her mouth, but she kept it there, swallowed it down. Ingrid didn't need this panic. After all, it was her future more than her mother's. "It's been hard," she concluded, "that's all, just hard."

It was dark in the kitchen at the back of the house, but neither moved to turn on a light. Then:

"You've done so much," Ingrid said in an unbelievably kind and patient voice. That was something her father, director of adult day care, must have passed on to her. She certainly didn't get it from her mother.

Claudia cleared her throat, switched on the lamp. "I'm sorry it's such a bummer here. You're probably never going to come back." She took a sip of the horrible herbal tea. "So. Tell me. What are your plans? Where are you and Sasha going next?" But before Ingrid could answer she said, "It's just been a little overwhelming. The drought, the emphysema, and now Arthur Wren and that VW bus. Where'd she get it? It must be thirty-five years old. Arthur had one exactly like it."

"Maybe it's his," Ingrid said.

"That would be too much. That would totally be too much." But even as Claudia said this, she knew that indeed that's where the bus came from. Those wealthy landowners in California. They would have garaged it and paid one of their Mexican laborers to fit it out with a rebuilt engine. That old box of metal. How their bodies had knocked into its tinny walls—arms, legs, feet—thrashing. She had trusted him. She hadn't even tried to cover up her happiness. Well, no more. And now the witness of her undoing had returned. The vessel of her lost life. Looking better than ever. Well, coincidence upon coincidence. Okay. But what was she supposed to do with it? What? She grew flowers and vegetable plants that she sold. That was enough.

Her daughter, who was not, after all, Arthur's daughter, hadn't said anything. Instead, she was rooting around in the olive green bag she'd taken out of the bus when they first drove up. She seemed to have found what she was looking for and plunked it onto the table. A CD. Actually, a clear plastic case with a CD inside of it.

Oh God, music. Silently she said please, no music. These kids were anachronisms all the way. Janis Joplin, Jimi Hendrix. That was who they listened to, her heroes. What was wrong with theirs? Out loud she said in her most poised and neutral voice, "What's this?" but she didn't pick it up.

"It's me and Sasha. We made it."

"Yeah?" She held it, looked at its unmarked silver face.

"Go ahead, play it. I want you to hear it."

Claudia was heading over to the counter when she remembered that she'd taken the combination radio-CD player out to
the greenhouse in May, when she was doing plant chores six,
eight hours a day. But the war news had so sickened her that
she'd turned it off and left it there. "The CD player's in the greenhouse. I guess I should bring it in," she said, reaching for the
flashlight, but reluctantly, because she didn't want to take this
next step, whatever it might be.

"Let's go out there," Ingrid said in a bright voice. "We can listen to it under the stars."

"It's going to be cold," Claudia offered.

But when Ingrid took her arm and walked her into the night,
it was still warm. The sky was so clear there were layers upon layers of stars, and the wide swath of the Milky Way stretched above
their heads like a pathway they might actually be able to ascend.
Ingrid found the pile of feedbags and spread them out on the
ground next to the greenhouse. Then she cranked open a window above where the radio sat, and they lay down outside. Claudia looked upward, but the stars were so profuse she couldn't
find her old standbys. Vega, Polaris, even the familiar shape of
Cassiopeia, where had they gone? Was the human race so entirely
lost, so entirely abandoned even *these* maps were missing?

For the first few minutes there was no sound at all. Maybe the
CD was corrupted, and they could simply lie there in silence.
But then a sound emerged, an accordion and a piano, and then,
after a while, harmonizing female voices. Okay, she thought,
kind of nice. Rising riffs, descending cascades, the piano crisp

and official. The piano was trying to assert order over everyone else, but the accordion would have none of it. It was passionate, helpless, squalling with abandon. Buoyed by the accordion, the voices, lovely but thin, gained density, became more certain. There were words, but she didn't even try to understand them. What were words except syllables that didn't communicate what the heart desired?

Now the voices gained. They took the challenge and came around to stand with the piano, harmonizing. If flowers could sing, these would be columbine, fragile and delicate, reaching upward only to drift away. The piano paused, and then the accordion came forward to solo.

Ingrid had played accordion. Along with the flute and violin, it had been one of the several instruments of her unremarkable high school career in marching band and orchestra.

Was this her now, this lonely but forceful pushing in and out of air, this musical breathing? The accordion was calling its friends, it called and called, but only later did a voice answer back. Wavering. Then the other came, strengthened it, and soon there was the piano too, rippling behind them. They had found each other. They were united again, singing the same sad melody they had started with, but now it was bigger, more terrible. Claudia felt herself swelling to enormous proportions. The minor key had located her sentries, and one by one, it was taking them out. She had no defenses. The accordion insisted. It squeezed under her ribcage, flowed up the ladder of her ribs, and spread out in her chest, pumping it full of all the things she'd closed her life to. It made her miss them so very much.

When the recording stopped, she turned on her side, toward

her daughter. She draped her arm over her waist and pressed into the soft, giving skin. "I'm so glad you're here!" she burst out. "It's beautiful, really beautiful. I mean, it's so sad it's more than beautiful." She was looking for the right word, which of course wasn't there. "It makes me feel . . . "

Hopeful. But how could that be?

Daily Life of the Pioneers

Ellie Mellie!" their mother called from the stairs, sending her voice up the three stories of the narrow Philadelphia house where the two girls lived with their mother, Beryl, and their father, Earl. *Ellie Mellie* blended the daughters into a single exotic and unfathomable creature, something that might squawk and squeal in a rainforest.

"You calling us Bellie?" the girls answered. They were building a structure out of wooden blocks on the floor of Eleanor's bedroom.

"Come down! I need your help!"

"In a minute!" Eleanor answered. "Coming!" Melinda shouted, but then they went back to their work, knowing their mother would go back to hers and the matter would be dropped. They were not the sort of daughters who helped with chores, and their parents, perennially distracted by matters more agreeable than the children creature, were not the sort of parents who insisted.

It was a democracy of sorts, almost a utopia. No one was in charge, and everyone had a nickname and did what they wanted. The permissions stretched and changed shape like a rubber band. The girls called their mother Bellie, which rhymed with their nicknames, or Booby, which referred to their mother's habit of parading around the house bare-chested, or sometimes Mama Mounds, names which lapped into a haunted place they could sometimes see at the end of the upstairs hall.

The father's nickname came from the land of the bathroom and was the result of a privacy creeping into the mouth and exploding in sputters and giggles. Such a term would never be spoken out loud in any other family. So there was a shiver of the dare in calling, "Hey Old Poop!" when they wanted their father's attention. The other male in the household was Old Fart, the dog, a grizzled, short-legged canine of indeterminate breed who shared understandings with the father. Two primarily: that going abroad into the world was a pleasure, the dog on his four legs, the father in his sports car, and that aging, though inevitable, should be denied. The dog's style was to eat grass and throw up. Earl's style was to practice cures he studied in health books.

These daughters were never punished for the disrespect they showed their parents, because this was not a household where punishment happened. Ellie and Mellie taunted their mother and father in front of acquaintances and friends, and each time they said, *Hey Booby Belly*, or *What do you want Old Poop*, everyone had a good laugh. But Eleanor and Melinda went into such paroxysms of laughter they pushed it up the scale to a manic pitch.

Not to mention how they ran around in costumes. They slept in the same clothes they played in day after day, and there certainly weren't any regular bedtimes, because the adults had an active social life. The daughters were dragged from one party to another where they danced, laughed, sang in outrageous and wild fashion, and were generally admired and loved for it.

Yet woven into the fabric of those halcyon days were patches of darkness. That's when their parents would do an about-face and institute rigor. Daily baths, for instance, and bedtimes before midnight. Of course, for Beryl and Earl, this was the ultimate challenge, but they did read the current authorities on rigor, and they did put their advice into practice, at least for a while.

One of these attempts happened during the spring of Melinda's disastrous second year in grade school. Eleanor, two years older at nine, was the more forward and articulate part of the children creature. So it was she that Beryl took aside to report in excited tones that the family was going to have an entirely new and wonderful adventure. Eleanor knew that when her mother used the word *adventure* it was to cover up selfish motives or a disagreeable plan. "I bet!" she said sarcastically. "Absolutely," Beryl proclaimed. "Each one of us is going to have a chance to experience our body's full potential."

Had Eleanor paid attention to the pile of paperbacks their father kept on the edge of the bathtub, she might have noticed a new one with a shiny cover: *The Alexander Technique or How to Restore Your Body to Its Original Perfection*. That book was going to throw a long shadow over their lives, but its immediate effect was a twice-weekly trip through the Philadelphia suburbs to meet with George and Polly Bersch, who ran a boarding school specializing in posture and diet, and in the evenings gave private lessons.

"Welcome, friends!" That first night George's raspy voice greeted them at the door. Eleanor was startled by the tall and skinny specter, and unable to see the top of him, stared at the space between his bowed legs. Here was an archway, child-sized. She was about to dart through it, imagining the adults' encouraging laughter, when all of a sudden George placed his skeletal hand on the top of her head and stilled the impulse. How dare he? She ducked out only to find that his hand had moved to her shoulder, where it stayed through the introductions.

The Scully family were instructed to remove their shoes before entering the room of impossibly bright and polished floors, and this caused some embarrassment for Beryl, because the girls' socks were hardly any cleaner than the soles of their shoes. "Take off your socks," she whispered. "Stuff them in your sneakers."

"But I don't want to go barefoot," Melinda whined. "I don't want to go . . . " she repeated in a louder voice, and Beryl, who didn't want a scene snapped, "All right. Keep your socks on then. Oh George," she crooned, "what an exquisite room this is. It feels simply spiritual, doesn't it, Earl? Simply spiritual, because you can see the dimensions and there's no clutter."

"Very nice, very nice," Earl muttered.

"Please help yourself to some healthful snacks." George indicated a table where they saw bowls of nuts, dried apricots, and a pitcher of water. "The girls can sit in these chairs, and Earl and

77

Beryl, we'll work on you first in the lesson room." He glided across the polished floor, their parents following him. "Mommy!" Melinda cried in a panic, but George looked at the children be-fore closing the door to the other room, and such clear and un-ambiguous power glistened in his long, narrow face that she went quiet. For the entire hour Eleanor and Melinda stayed in the area he'd appointed them to and behaved.

The wait was over when Eleanor heard Beryl's exclamations. "That was simply wonderful. I feel renewed, revived, completely different. You are masterful, you two. Let me go over it again. I just say it to myself, and I don't even think about trying to make it happen, because I want the intention to be pure. Is that right?"

"Don't *try* to do," a woman's voice instructed. "Just *do*."

"Just do. Well, that should be easy enough. Don't you think, Earl? Just do."

"Just do," Earl repeated. "Just do."

Now the door was open and their mother's voice was louder. "So completely wonderful." She gave George and Polly each a hug, while Earl disengaged himself and came over to the chil-dren's corner. He whispered, "It's very nice. You'll like them."

"I'm hungry," Melinda whispered back. "Me too," Eleanor said in her regular voice, and were it an ordinary day, their com-plaints would have crescendoed into a wild stomp. But George had turned in their direction, and once again, Eleanor saw the chill of his eyes and stopped, and when she stopped Melinda stopped too. They followed George back to the lesson room.

Eleanor's first glimpse of Polly was her first exposure to the narrow world of the ascetic. For the entire lesson, she studied this species of woman she'd never seen before. Though Polly was not as tall as George, she was just as thin, and everything that made her a woman, the breasts and hips that Beryl had in such abundance, was minimized. Her body was a wisp, a feather, and her voice was no stronger. Yet when she touched Eleanor it was quick and penetrating, and Eleanor could feel it all the way to her bone.

"Drop your shoulders," Polly said, guiding Eleanor into a chair.

Next to her, George was doing the same with Melinda.

Eleanor tried to drop her shoulders, and Polly said, "Don't try. Just let your body do it on its own." Next to them, George put a finger on the top of Melinda's head and said, "Stand up."

"I will if you take your finger off me," she said.

"Stand up," he repeated just as quietly with his finger still on her head, and Eleanor, who was watching everything in the mirror that reflected the two chairs, the two girls, and the two teachers, saw Melinda stand up. "Good," George said crisply. His finger stayed right there on the top of Melinda's head as he had her walk. In the mirror her sister was knees, elbows, and a cloud of wild hair.

"You're so lucky," Beryl once told her in private. "You got your father's blond hair and his beautiful blue eyes."

Melinda, seated again, staring without expression into the mirror, was not lucky. She had inherited the brown eyes and black hair of Beryl's family, Russian Jews who had escaped the pogroms and settled in New York at the turn of the century.

"Drop your shoulders," George said. Melinda's face didn't change. "Drop your shoulders," George said again in exactly the same tone of voice.

She frowned. "That's what I'm doing!"

"Don't do. Resist the impulse to use intention. Melinda . . . " but he didn't go on; he paused. "It's important that you listen to me. Now, once again, resist the impulse to use intention."

Melinda's eyes froze. Eleanor could tell that in a moment her sister was going to explode. "We don't understand those words," she explained quickly.

"It doesn't matter. Her body is listening. It knows what I'm asking it to do. There you go!" he said suddenly. "Okay. Fine."

"Your body knows everything," Polly explained at Eleanor's back. "And as long as you don't interfere, it will take good care of you. Your body always knows the right way. That's why babies have perfect posture. But give them a few years, things will go crooked. We believe that with a few simple measures we can undo the effects of all the shame and distress human beings create. Especially when we work with them as children." She paused, cupping Eleanor's head in her hands and turning it forward. "Look at me in the mirror. See me from the point of vision which is here." She marked the place with a finger at the back of her head. "Let your mind be empty of thought. Okay. Fine."

What was shameandistress, Eleanor wondered.

At the lesson next week they graduated to lying on massage tables. Polly placed a stack of books on each side of Eleanor's hips, folded one leg up, and put her hand over the toes on the other so the heat of her fingers penetrated. "I wish my neck to be free. Go ahead, say it to yourself after me. To go forward and up, to lengthen and widen my back." Eleanor repeated the strange sentences to herself and shifted her position according to Polly's instructions.

In preparation for that lesson, Beryl had taken the girls shopping, and there were clean white socks on their feet. They submitted to new socks and then the lessons, but it might have been because Earl promised to treat everyone to hamburgers and sodas afterward, or it might have been because the austere methods of the Berschs were so antithetical to the lavish indulgences of home, it *was* an adventure after all.

So Eleanor didn't feel worried when Beryl announced that the girls would attend the Berschs' summer camp. Only Melinda did.

"Why?" she asked.

"Six weeks of a pure and natural environment will be good for you. You'll live in the woods just like the pioneer children, and there won't be sweets or animal food. Your diet will be raw vegetables, which are very tasty and very healthy, and there won't be toys or books."

"Why?" Melinda said.

"Because sweetie. We live in a very polluted world. The Berschs are people who are sensitive to that. What they want is for you children to experience a natural life. It's an experiment, and I think we're all very lucky that the Berschs agreed to include you with their full-time boarding students. It's an opportunity. The Berschs know exactly what you need and exactly what's good for you. Imagine that. And you know what else?"

"I'm not going," Melinda said.

But Beryl, busy exuding, didn't pay attention. "Let me explain something to you. Television, processed foods, and that's not all.

The Berschs think that the reason you're having that trouble in school, honey, you know, the special reading class they put you in? It's milk. What other animal drinks infant food after it's weaned? You're drinking food that nature intended for baby cows. But you're not a cow. So it slows you down, it makes you sleepy, and that's why all of a sudden this year school has been so hard. The Berschs think that six weeks without milk, without any animal food at all, we'll see vast and amazing improvement. I'm so excited. Six weeks being pioneer children, children who don't drink milk, with those kind and wonderful people. You'll be together, you'll have each other, and Daddy and I will be sending our love."

Two weeks later the black Rambler merged into a line of cars on the highway and bypassed all of Philadelphia and its suburbs, taking the daughters deep into wild Pennsylvania landscape, distant and strange. Many hours later, Earl steered the car down a dirt road, turned onto a rutted path, and parked at a clearing where three tents and a school bus were stationed. They had a tearful goodbye. The girls stood with their suitcases on a trampled piece of ground and watched the silver fins disappear into the vegetation, dirt peppering the back window, obscuring the heads of the two imperfect people they loved most in the world.

Camp life started immediately. They were introduced to Noelle, an older camper, who was also one of the wintertime boarding students. She was twelve and had hair so straight it looked ironed and eyes so dark and unreflecting they were polished stones. The three of them were the only girls, so Noelle was also their tent mate. Polly slept in the school bus that served as the kitchen and first aid station. The grassy area next to the school bus, shaded by a tarp that stretched from the roof of the bus to two trees, was the dining area. On one side, George shared a tent with the oldest boy. Then there were two thirteen-year-old boys; they had the tent next to George's. The girls' tent was on the other side of the dining room under an evergreen.

While they were setting up, unrolling sleeping bags, making stacks of clothing, George ducked into their new home and gave them a porta potty, a deep yellow basin with a lid, which he suggested they keep in the back so it wouldn't get knocked over. It had to be emptied and washed out every day. That chore was to be performed with an agreeable disposition, and should there be evidence of it being performed otherwise, the camper would be required to do a double turn. "Cleaning the potty is not a reason to get squeamish or silly. It's merely one of many chores here at camp."

That was how the six weeks of purity began. For a place that didn't have any activities, like boating, archery, or horseback riding, the Berschs kept them busy. The campers prepared meals, cleaned up afterward, and attended to daily hygiene. For daily hygiene, each camper had an aluminum bucket that held enough water to last all day. They washed their faces in the morning with it and brushed their teeth. It was also to be their washing water at night.

There was one activity related to pleasure: eating apples before going to sleep. According to the Berschs, apples had a dental cleansing property, and campers who ate one after dinner were excused from the nighttime brushing of teeth. So it wasn't entirely a rigid system. But one relaxed rule didn't mean that the other rules were not firm. For instance, if they happened to spill their water, they couldn't go back to the stream for more. It was easy to spill on the path to the tent area. Or during the day, if they kept their water bucket in a public place, someone ended up walking into it. Melinda always lost hers climbing the hill above the stream. So most of the time Eleanor's water had to be enough for her, too.

Every evening, just before going to bed, the entire camp community of eight people walked down the path to a field. At a signal from George, they bent over and brushed their hair a hundred strokes. Even the boys. Noelle's shiny strands dripped to the ground like water. Then everyone stood up, hair wild about their faces (except Noelle's, which draped neatly over her shoulders), and faced the disappearing sun to say their Alexander, the same odd phrases Polly used to have Eleanor say to herself at the lesson:

I wish my neck to be free
My head to go forward and up
To lengthen and widen my back.

On the fifth day Eleanor was jolted awake. Light shrilled at the tent door, birds called in alarm. Melinda and Noelle slept calmly on either side of her. But something had nagged at Eleanor during the night, something she'd forgotten. Now, with her eyes open and dawn pushing through the canvas, she couldn't remember what it was.

Melinda. It had to do with Melinda. Melinda, who was only seven, who hadn't wanted to come to camp. Melinda couldn't understand things as well as Eleanor; she was too young. "Your job is to take care of your sister," Earl said. The problem was this. Melinda ate the nuts and seeds they were given at breakfast, she ate the raw leaves they were given at lunch, but she wasn't eating the uncooked vegetables at dinner. Would she starve or get malnutrition? Malnutrition like the Unicef children on the posters at school, big bellies and enormous eyes?

Every morning before breakfast, the younger boys set up traytables in the dining area. The boy named Dirt was pouring sunflower seeds onto everyone's tabletop and, from another bag, counting out ten almonds.

Eleanor's job was to open the folding chairs, wipe them off, and place them at each table. When Noelle walked up, Polly asked if they had washed their hands. "Yes," they said, and after that Eleanor said, "The birds woke me up. " Noelle said, "Oh, you'll get used to it," and Polly said, "Isn't it lovely?" *Not exactly*, Eleanor could have answered, because the birds were messengers, not entertainers. But could she follow that with, *Melinda's going to starve?*

Polly was sitting at her tray-table. "My sister," Eleanor began, except she could tell she didn't have Polly's attention. "Melinda doesn't . . . ," she tried again, but something warned her to stop. Maybe it was George rising to his feet. He faced the circle of traytables, where all the other campers were already eating, and in a soft and pleasant voice said, "May I remind everyone that when our bodies are receiving sustenance in its most vital and available uncooked form, it is necessary that our entire attention be directed to chewing. No talking please. Our task at each meal is only to chew. Chew slowly. Chew thoroughly. Be attentive to this important first step of the digestive process."

Eleanor returned to her tray-table. She could feel George's gaze settle on her, so she ate a nut and then a seed, picking each one up separately and chewing until they were pulp. That activity lasted through the entire breakfast.

The next activity was filling their water buckets. The path to the stream was steep and rocky; there were pricker bushes leaning over it, grabbing their arms. Once in the water, each camper jumped from rock to rock to a small pool where the stream spilled down from a higher level and a bucket placed under the top stone rang with splashing water. Most of the campers performed this chore without wetting their clothes or their shoes, but Eleanor and Melinda got soaked every time. Their legs were shorter, their jumps not as confident. On hot mornings the soaking was nice, but on the cool days it made them cold.

On the second week of the Berschs' summer camp the weather turned soggy. Melinda's wet feet gave her a chill. It was her turn to clean the potty, so when she didn't come to breakfast, George got up and strode to their tent. Even though Eleanor's attention *was* truly placed on the first step of the process of digesting a walnut, she left her tray-table and caught up just as George was lifting the tent flap. He asked politely, "Why are you still in the tent? Your chore is waiting for you. And you're late for breakfast."

"I don't feel good," Melinda replied in a weak voice. "My throat hurts."

Eleanor peeped in behind George and saw her sister bury her

face in the pillow. That was part of the performance. They each had a repertoire of symptoms that so confounded their parents they always let them miss school just in case they were actually sick. But George had consulted the work schedule; he knew it was potty day for Melinda. Still, she put on a convincing show. She made her eyelids heavy, her forehead glisten. Even her curls seemed different. "You will get up, get dressed, and only after you've cleaned the potty will you be allowed at breakfast. But be quick about it, because everyone is waiting."

"I can't get up," Melinda groaned. That groan was Melinda's specialty, and this one, Eleanor thought, was the best ever. Plus the way she suddenly tossed the sleeping bag off as though she were burning up!

"Each camper shares in basic maintenance. With an agreeable disposition. All the time and for every chore. So get your shovel and your potty. We will wait for you at breakfast."

Melinda's eyes were closed tight. Her eyelids looked purple. How did she make her eyelids purple?

"Do you want me to help you?" Eleanor's voice shot out from behind George's knees. "I could stay and help you."

"Yes," Melinda whispered, but her eyes were still closed.

"Okay. Fine. Your sister has been kind enough to offer her help. But you must get up now." George unzipped the tent flap, flooding the sleeper with light, and left.

"Hey!" Eleanor whispered as soon as they were alone. "Aren't you going to get up?"

Melinda turned to her side.

Their mother checked for fever by pressing her cheek to their foreheads. Checking for fever was the first signal that a performance had been convincing. So Eleanor dropped down to all fours and pressed her face against her sister's. Even before their skin touched, she knew that Melinda was burning up. "This isn't pretend," she said gravely. Were they at home she would stomp and shout till an adult came to take over, but here, where she was afraid to ask even the simplest question, she stayed quiet. "Look, I'll get you up and I'll do your chore for you, but we have to make it look like you're doing it. Okay? Then you'll have to come to breakfast. And then we can tell him. We'll tell him together. You're sick. You need to stay in bed. But right now, you have to get out of it." She pulled at Melinda's arms, lifted at her armpits, and had her standing. Then she found her sneakers and put her feet into them without bothering to tie the laces. "You carry the potty when we leave the tent. I'll carry the shovel." Melinda's hair stood up as though it were electrified, and even though she was out of bed her eyes had an inward look that made Eleanor wonder if she could see anything at all. As she picked the potty up by the handle, it tipped. But the lid latched tightly so nothing slopped out, and by the second week the stench was hardly worth the trouble it took for the girls to pinch their noses and say *pee-you!* Pioneers didn't say pee-you. That signified a disagreeable disposition. Pioneers said, *Okay. Fine.*

As Melinda ducked through the flap, Eleanor came behind. Everyone in the dining area looked up, but because their attention was on the first step of the digestive process, no one said a word. However, Eleanor thought Polly looked startled.

Eleanor guided Melinda to the right fork in the path. It took them around the school bus, down a hill, and behind an enormous tree to the compost. The compost was a pit four feet deep and four feet across. Next to it there was a pile of decaying leaves.

Both the pit and the leaf pile had been there for many years, George had told them, the pit refreshed each summer from the various groups that used the property, and the leaf pile refreshed each fall with new rakings. The campers were instructed to shovel a layer of leaves over each potty deposit so the metabolic process could be facilitated. George had explained the metabolic process. He'd told them that the leaf pile was a digesting organism just like their bodies. It was alive just as they were, and that's why, if a camper stuck her hand into the center, it was grabbed by dampness and heat. Eleanor loosened a layer of leaves with her shovel, but then she reached in with her bare hands to touch this living organism and lift into light a clump of hot, moldering material. "Just spill it," she told Melinda, who teetered on the edge of the pit still holding the potty. "Go ahead," she said gently. But Melinda, who wasn't seeing anything, took a step forward, offering the potty up in a manner George would have approved of, and tripped over her laces. Eleanor screamed. The lid bounced off the potty as it hit the ground, and the contents splattered on Melinda's face because she had reached the bottom of the pit at exactly the same moment the potty did.

She sank down, her arms flailing, splattering clumps of things in all directions. "Keep your mouth closed!" Eleanor shouted. "Don't go down! Please! Hold your head up!"

George did finally arrive, but when? It felt like hours. He waded into the thick slurry, and pulled the feverish child out. After that there was a bath in the stream, a hair washing at the waterfall, and fresh clothes. At day's end, Melinda was tucked into a temporary bed in Polly's room in the school bus. Her head was propped up on two pillows, and her body was draped with a sheet. Polly applied a cool rag to her forehead every half hour and told Eleanor not to worry.

"My mother always gives her aspirin. That brings the fever down."

"We want the fever. It's beneficial. It's the human animal's way of throwing off the toxins. This lavender water is very soothing," Polly said. "She'll be fine. See how well she's sleeping?"

Melinda's face was white. Her breath was shallow. The ancient groan escaped from her lips and her thick hair, even though it was clean, looked just as electrified as it had that morning. Eleanor stared at her sister, preparing a sentence she was scared to say out loud, repeating it to herself in the hope that one of the repetitions would simply, by itself, transform into sound. But while she was waiting for that to happen Polly said, "She'll be fine. Your help is needed at dinner. Go. I'll keep good watch."

"I think you should call my parents." There! It came out.

"I know you love your sister very much. But there isn't a phone here. You know that. Now go ahead. She'll be fine."

Eleanor picked up Melinda's small, hot hand, squeezed it, and said, "But she's never had a fever this high. She's never been sick like this." In fact, Eleanor couldn't remember a single illness either had suffered which wasn't, in some way, performed.

The next day, George made a short speech. "Pioneer children helped their parents with the tasks of daily life. The girls helped with child care, washing of clothes, and sewing. The boys worked with the animals and out in the fields and the woods. Modern pioneers," George told them, "will do everything together, so everyone will receive the same knowledge and experience." The campers carried their soiled clothes down to the stream, where George handed out bars of brown soap and showed them how to scrub the garments against the rocks. The articles he demonstrated with were the shorts and shirt Melinda had soiled. Eleanor watched to make sure he soaped them thoroughly so all traces of the metabolic process would be cleansed away.

Washing clothes took up the whole morning. So did gathering jewelweed. That's what they did on another day. Polly showed them how to mash the plant into a pulp and mix it with oil. Then they pressed the pulp into glass jars, which they stored in the darkness under the bus. They would use it as salve for poison ivy and bug bites.

"How's your sister?" Dirt asked.

They had put their jars away, and now they stood in the shade next to the bus. "I don't know."

"Haven't you seen her?"

"They won't let me. She's contagious for five days."

"She's still on the bus, isn't she?" He put a finger to his lips and then quickly stooped down, crouching low enough to scuttle out of sight under the bus. Eleanor followed. On the other side, away from the campers, they stood up. He beckoned her to Polly's end and stooped down, holding his hands clasped. "I'll give you a hoist."

Eleanor didn't know what a hoist was.

"Put your foot here. Hold on here." She did as she was told, and before she knew what was happening, he had lifted her high enough to see in the windows. "Is she there?"

She saw the bed. But where was Melinda? Was that pale tiny face on the pillow her sister? It couldn't be. The hair was gone. Eleanor tapped the pane, but the face didn't move, and the body under the sheet was completely still.

Dead. But not only dead, bald. The words rode in the forefront of her mind and condensed into a short phrase: dead *and* bald. That outrage became the rhythm that accompanied her movements. Dead *and* bald. She wiped the tray-tables to it, opened them up to it, arranged them in the half-circle to it. But then she didn't sit down. She couldn't. Instead, she went to stand by Polly and waited to get her attention, reminding herself that in pioneer times, alive became dead often. It was part of the metabolic process of the earth itself, as George was always telling them in regard to vegetable peelings, potty matter, and expired insects. But she missed Melinda. And she was supposed to have taken care of her. Plus there was the special reading class, which after a whole year hadn't taught her to read. Would six weeks of no milk do it instead? Melinda had to be alive to supply the answer.

While Polly was giving instructions to one of the boys, Eleanor practiced a question: *She's too big for the compost pit isn't she?* It was a combination of two questions she was wondering about: Why did she have to die? And what will we do with her now that she is? But she lost courage when Polly turned to her.

"She's much better," Polly said. "Probably tomorrow she'll be back at the tent. She needs to have a whole day without fever. Then she can return."

"She's alive?" Eleanor asked. There wasn't any need to rehearse that.

"Better than before," Polly told her.

Then an unrehearsed sentence popped out: "Why did you cut her hair?"

Polly's face showed surprise. But she covered it quickly. "I guess it's hard for sisters to stay apart, isn't it? Let's hope you haven't contracted her sickness. I'm going to explain why cutting her hair was necessary, but you may not understand. So all I can offer is my promise that she has received the healthy and natural care that her sickness asked us to give her."

"Aspirin?" Eleanor asked.

"Herbs," Polly said. "Teas and poultices. And the removal of her hair because it weighed her down. It made her tired. The light couldn't get through. You see, all her old habits were locked up in that ancient tangle, and she needed to leave her old habits behind if she was going to get well. That's the reason. Now go ahead, everyone's waiting for you so we can begin our evening meal."

Melinda did return the next day. She was very thin, and without any hair she looked as unhealthy as the dark-skinned child in the Unicef poster that had hung in Eleanor's classroom all year long, silently showing the children what would happen if they didn't eat all of their lunch. The Berschs excused her from potty duty. Forever. She also wouldn't ever again have to get her own water. That task was assigned to Dirt. Because he was strong, he could manage two buckets of water at once. That meant he came to their tent every morning to get her bucket and, after the water chore, to return it. "Atta boy," he said as he set it down next to Eleanor and Noelle's buckets. Eleanor couldn't figure out what

Atta Boy meant, but it seemed like a kind thing, and in those long, hot weeks when no one laughed or joked, and play was never indulged in, *Atta Boy* seemed like a happy sound.

On the first day she was back, Eleanor hugged Melinda five times, not all at once, but throughout the day, when she felt like it. Life suddenly took on the same amazement as Melinda in her recovered state. Things startled her with beauty: a tree, a black-eyed Susan in a field, even a raw string bean sitting on her tray-table. "I love you," Eleanor said that first night, bundled in her sleeping bag and stretching out like an enormous earthworm to hug Melinda a sixth time. "I'll always love you no matter what."

On the second day of Melinda's return from the dead, life went back to normal. She helped Polly at the school bus while the other campers went down to the stream. "Why do they call you Dirt?" Eleanor asked the older boy when they were standing next to the lip of stone over which the stream flung itself tirelessly, splashing into as many buckets as they offered up.

"Dirt? Like dirty?"

"Isn't that your name?"

He laughed. "K at the end. Like smirk. Like irk."

Smirk and irk were words she didn't know so she asked, "How old are you anyway?"

"Sixteen. Too old for this place, don't you think?"

"Yeah," she said. "Me and Melinda are too young."

The next week everyone had poison ivy. Polly collected the jars under the bus and gave one to each camper. They applied the green salve thickly and often, and one evening, facing six painted pioneers, George made a speech about pestilence and drought. In Africa those were the conditions all the time. There, in lush and fertile Pennsylvania, they should welcome poison ivy as a test of will power. "If you give in and scratch, you'll lose. If you abstain and leave your rash alone, the gift of health will be yours."

That night, Eleanor patted her rash, brushing it softly with the tips of her fingers in a friendly, reassuring way, a beneficial for the toxin rather than the angry scratching she could hear Melinda indulge in on the other side of the tent. Only Noelle slept soundly.

The next morning, Eleanor's belly was a topographical map, a mountainous continent criss-crossed with rivers of pus. Melinda's map was on the back of her legs, behind her knees, a thin hilly country stretching down to her ankles. Her eyes filled with tears. "When are we going home?" she asked.

"I don't know. No one's told us."

"I want to go home," Melinda whimpered, dragging her nails down her itchy legs. "Let's call them."

"You can't," Noelle said firmly. "Don't you know that by now? There's no telephone, no mailboxes, no electricity, no running water. We don't live in the regular world here, and that means we can't talk to our parents, because they do. We can't even send them postcards. Haven't you noticed they don't really approve of our parents?"

"I want to go home," Melinda whispered softly.

"That's exactly why they don't want you contacting them. My first year, I tried to run away. But George brought me back, and he explained everything to me, and now I'm glad to be at school. Because my mom's really sick. She's sick in the head and she's sick in the body."

"But our parents aren't sick. And they can give us medicine."

"Medicine only makes you sicker. All these things they make us do, strange as they seem, keep us healthy. The other things, the things they do in the world out there, don't. That's why my mother got sick in the head and that's why she's sick in the body. The medicines hurt her. And your parents, I'm sorry to say, are probably as sick as my mom. They can't help it. It's milk, but it's also other things, and medicine is part of that."

All day long the foreign continents on Eleanor and Melinda's bodies were covered with such a thick application of salve the rash was conquered. Jewelweed seemed to work after all. None of the other pioneers were scratching either, and George was jubilant. On the spot, he offered to take the campers on a tree identification walk and gave Eleanor and Melinda the front of the line as their reward for mature forbearance in the face of nature's challenge. They stopped in front of a slender tree with a shaggy trunk and George said, "This is hop hornbeam. It grows slowly, and in young woods like these the trunks are always narrow. And there's a red maple. It's a fast growing tree. It's called red maple not because its leaves are red, you can see they're a beautiful deep green color, but because in the winter, when the tree is bare, you can see the red tips of each tiny branch. They're so red that if the sun is behind them, the whole tree has a red halo."

They walked onward. Suddenly, George clapped his hands in excitement. "Ah, here's one of my favorites. Striped maple. A funny little tree, isn't it? Look at the thin, striped trunk, the enormous floppy leaves."

What Eleanor couldn't figure out was how the Berschs got six kids to believe in their program. Even Melinda had become agreeable. At that very moment she was standing by the striped maple, touching the bark and listening to George. So maybe the old habits did die. Maybe light did clear them out. Now every morning, Noelle brushed Melinda's hair, making sure the fuzz growing out of her scalp was tangle-free.

At week six there was a new development.

"It's called tahini sauce," Polly said.

Each camper had a cup of it. But it wasn't to drink, it was a dip for their vegetables. Even so, what Melinda didn't use as a dip she drank when no one was looking, and at dinner she asked if she could have more of it.

Polly said, "Any goodness, if in excess, turns to greed."

"You mean I can't?" Melinda asked sweetly.

"Tomorrow at lunch. Not till then. And then, only a small amount."

"Why?" Melinda asked, not understanding.

"It's fat and salt. Necessary, but in small amounts only."

There were three more days of camp after the day of tahini sauce. On each one of them, a cup holding a small amount of the tan liquid was available at the noon meal. Though Melinda was the most vocal about her desire for more, all the campers appreciated the rich taste. George explained that a healthy diet was a balance of fat and lean, salt and sweet, that moderation was the guiding principle. "Excess should at all costs be avoided." He made that statement at a lunch that consisted of carrot strips and tahini sauce.

The next morning they didn't fill their buckets down at the

stream. After the breakfast clean-up, they climbed into a van that had mysteriously appeared in the little clearing. They traveled down the dirt road, all the places Eleanor knew from their walks flying by. Once they turned onto the paved road, she was surprised to see other cars. How could there be a traffic light, how could there be a parking lot? How could there be that woman coming out of the supermarket with grocery bags? It was the other world, unmistakable; it hadn't changed. There was even a gallon of milk in her cart. The campers were horrified to see her pick it up and put it into her trunk. Didn't she know?

They waited in the van while George went into the market. Like anyone else, as though he did it every day. He returned with one small grocery bag and drove to a park. Everyone piled out, and soon it became clear that the pioneers were going to have a picnic. George led them to a table far away from the other picnics, from shouts and laughter, and the odors of grilled meat. Polly assigned tasks. She gave Eleanor the job of counting out paper plates. Melinda passed out napkins. Once they were seated, George stood up and addressed them all.

"Our experiment in pure and direct experience will come to an end tomorrow morning. This is our goodbye banquet. It is my hope that each and every camper will continue to eat raw vegetables and be a good example for your parents and friends. It is my hope that the evening practice of brushing your hair and saying your Alexander will be continued by each and every one of you. I know my boarding students will do it, and I hope that the Scully children will as well."

Eleanor looked straight ahead, thinking of home, trying to remember it. What Melinda did, she couldn't tell.

Then with a flourish, George set the paper bag on the table and took out five boxes of frozen lima beans. One swipe of his plastic knife cut through the picture that showed hot steaming beans in a beautiful serving bowl with a pat of butter melting on the top. George opened the waxy cover and tried to knife through a still-frozen glob. But it was too hard, so he simply tore the beans apart with his fingers and put a frosty clump in the center of each plate. After they were passed around, George intoned a blessing. "May we enjoy these fruits of the earth on our final special day together. Suck till they're thawed campers, and then don't forget to chew!"

The next morning the black Rambler appeared at the forest clearing. Two fat, sweaty people stepped from the car. The woman wore a tight red dress and high-heeled shoes. "Where is everyone?" she cried. The tents were gone, all the other children had been taken away, and the dining area was dismantled. George and Polly were busy in the schoolbus; they hadn't heard the last parents drive up.

Eleanor stood with Melinda under the evergreen.

"Ellie Mellie!" the woman called. "Ellie Mellie!" But then her tone changed. "Oh my god, Earl, look at them, oh my god, they've been starved, they're skeletons!"

For the rest of their lives, certain phrases were a revolving door to that faraway summer, like digestive process, like agreeable disposition. "I can't talk now," Melinda said years later, laughing wickedly at a family dinner. "I'm concentrating on the first step of the digestive process." They were safely grown up, each with two children they'd been careful to treat as individuals and this was their annual feast for the uninhibited, a July celebration of the earth's bounty for the sisters and their families. The table before them was heaped with food. None of it had been prepared with milk products. There was home-raised chicken, potatoes and vegetables from the garden, pudding with a rich sauce. Around Eleanor's farmhouse the old fields had grown up in red maple; hop hornbeam flourished in the woods. Every season, she gathered jewelweed and turned it into salve.

"Way too much to eat!" Melinda cried. "All I need is a couple of almonds El, and a leaf of parsley. Remember that next time, okay?" At age thirteen, she'd been diagnosed with dyslexia. Now she was a graphic artist. Reaching over the mounds of food for the platter with chicken, silver bracelets tinkling on her freckled arm, she gave herself a generous helping. "Where'd the gravy go? Who's hiding it, come on guys." For Melinda, the summer with the Berschs had no complications. She'd let out a yelp and run into their mother's arms, laughing and crying and clinging to her greedily.

But Eleanor had stayed where she was under the evergreen. Clarity was too seductive. That was the problem with fanatics. It would be days before the rules became irrelevant, a week before she could go out in the summer evenings simply to play.

The Yes Column

Charlotte was an overachiever fresh from the New York state public education system, a strategist for multiple choice standardized tests who could memorize facts certified by the Board of Regents and then darken the correct bubbles on the answer sheets so that her answer sheet matched perfectly the computer prototype. In her non-academic life she was a finger acrobat who could instant message, listen to music, and shop on the Internet all at the same time. Rap, funk, and hip hop syncopated most everything she did, and now, at the end of high school, their steady percussions underscored her impatience to escape the small town she had lived in all her life.

Charlotte's twin brother got a scholarship at the University of Oregon. He bought a truck with a camper top on eBay so he could take his time and drive across the country. It seemed so simple. Charlotte wanted a faraway college too, but an easy one. She was tired of feeding the monster of education in Albany. She was tired of cramming facts, writing essays. She didn't want to think about thesis sentences. And she was especially tired of the boring topics they gave you: *What is the purpose of a college education? Describe the ways your senior year prepared you.* Charlotte wanted to plunge into raw unorganized existence. She wanted to explore beyond the answer bubbles, go to places where there were no facts at all. She wanted immersion. She wanted the drippy wet mess of doubt and confusion so she could track wet footprints all over the floors. Wasn't it time to be bold and heartless? Wasn't it time to consider a thesis sentence worth writing about? Here was one she and her brother might tackle! *There was no solution to the problem of their father's lover.* Yes! And the only way to save themselves was to get far away from the disaster of their parents' marriage.

The application to Juliette Gordon Low was one of the few that didn't require an essay. Even art schools, something she considered briefly, required them. She was such an expert at delivering right answers it took her no more than thirty minutes to complete, and although it was not the kind of school her father would have approved of, she stamped the envelope and sent it off. When the letter arrived in April from the Office of Admissions accepting her with a partial scholarship and the rest of the tuition covered by loans, she signed in the Yes column before thinking about it too deeply. The ethnic adventure presented by a women's college in a town in southern Georgia appealed to her Northern fantasies. She didn't discuss it with her father, an academic in their small upstate town, and she didn't discuss it with her mother, either. The only person she showed it to was her brother, who dubbed it with his general all-around word of approval: "sweet!" He was the one who forged their mother's signature on the check for the deposit, just as he had done on the check for the application. They decided that was their prerogative in a family where the parents were preoccupied. So it wasn't until their mother tripped over the New Student Orientation Packet, a bulky package sitting on the doorstep because it was too large for the mail slot, that the children's prerogative encountered at last the maternal force.

In the end, she wasn't angry about the forged checks. She wasn't angry about the choice of college. She was hurt. And this latest hurt on top of the wound caused by their father made her cry. The twins, separately and together, tried to justify and explain. But there was no undoing it. That her eighteen-year-old daughter had made a life-changing decision and accepted a long-term financial burden without even mentioning it to the adult she lived with was a fact.

And so it was fact that a month after her brother's departure, her mother woke her up at four a.m. to drive her to the airport in Buffalo. Charlotte stood on the curb next to their car, the sky beyond the parking garage streaked with the dusky yellows of a polluted dawn, the loudspeaker announcing departures. Looking at her mother's gaunt cheeks, she reached through the car window to touch her hand. "I'm sorry," she said. But her mother couldn't meet her eyes; she was crying. Charlotte said firmly, "You know what? I'm not going. I'll live at home with you and get a job. I'll pay you back for the deposit and the plane ticket and everything." But her mother wiped her face, put on the expression she'd worn in the last few weeks, chin up, mouth stretched wide and tight, a parody of a smile that would fool no one, said quickly, "I love you," and drove away.

All that day the planes stayed in the air and their brakes worked on the runways. Surprised and rumpled, Charlotte arrived. The tarmac glistened with wet heat and the airport, in the middle of a field with some kind of crop planted in it, was not only an airport but a cocktail lounge that permeated the baggage area with the smell of stale beer. The old man at the bar was also the cab driver, and as soon as Charlotte's bag showed up, he offered his services. She wasn't sure if Juliette Gordon Low College was the same thing he called Girls State, so on the drive past miles of identical fields she was nervous. But then she saw the sign and then the old trees and the plantation-style buildings from the catalogue. It didn't look like "two hundred acres of gracious Southern landscape"; it looked worn and ragged. Standing on the sidewalk, surrounded by her luggage, she was digging around in her purse for a couple of dollars when he drove away. That was the second time in one day a car left before she was completely ready.

She parked her luggage on the sagging porch of the great white antebellum mansion and went into the foyer. There were photographs chronicling the college's history, placards announcing various dedications, but none of them revealed the identity of its namesake. Wandering from item to item, hoping that

someone would come up and tell her where to go, Charlotte concluded that Juliette Gordon Low was a person the college was
embarrassed to honor, maybe a landowner who had lots of
slaves, or the unmarried daughter of a Confederate general. She
was thinking her brother would enjoy that irony when someone
giggled behind her. "Charlotte? Those your bags out there on the
veranda?"

"Is that a problem?"

"No problem. Just wondered if it was really you. Because you
know what?" the voice asked breathlessly.

As Charlotte turned to look at the other woman, she felt the
weight of all the miles she'd traveled, all the airport lounges
she'd sat in, and knew she was tired. She also knew that any person as sunny and eager as this face in front of her wouldn't understand even an iota of those things Charlotte considered
important.

"I'm Stacey, your roommate!" and before Charlotte could step
away, she wrapped her chubby arms around her and squeezed. "I
just knew! Someone said, that freshman from up north? She's
over in Administration. So I thought to myself, Charlotte's from
New York, and I ran right over!"

They rolled the suitcases across the parking lot and up the
stairs into a squat, colorless building. Stacey had already deco-
rated her portion of the small cinder block room. There were
posters of puppies and sunflowers, flouncy curtains on the window, and everything from the rug to the desk lamp was yellow.

That first night when Stacey was arranged on her matching
sheet set wearing a crisp summer nightgown, while Charlotte
was on top of her ragged cotton blanket in one of her brother's

discarded tee shirts, the fan made talking difficult. Still, Stacey attempted. Charlotte could tell that the actuality of the room-mate she'd been fantasizing about since April was far from satis-factory, but Stacey was from the old life, where making an effort mattered, so she didn't give up.

Crossing her legs, looking with curiosity at Charlotte's scat-tered belongings, all of them black or grey, nothing new or shiny, she asked, "You homesick?"

Charlotte pulled the huge shirt over her knees. It wasn't home she was homesick for, because home had disappeared. It was life before the lover. So, feeling like a refugee from some small, un-known east European country, with her long uneven dark hair and memories of difficult times, she laughed and tried to affect an easy tone. "For that place? No way. I'm glad I escaped."

"It was that bad?" Stacey asked and Charlotte, who was reluc-tant to reveal any more, steered the question away from anything too personal. "How would you feel if your dad came up to you on the day he was moving out and said, 'Cheer up. Life is absurd. That's the *only* thing a person can count on.' Great news, isn't it, really great news." She knew she sounded bitter, but that was how she and her brother had talked, and now, miles away from him, it felt good to do it again. "It was like I'm just one of his phi-losophy students. Never occurred to him even once that I *am* his daughter."

Her brother would have agreed with everything she was say-ing, plus added a dark and cynical thought of his own. Stacey said, "Now that you're here, you won't have to give that horrible business even five minutes of your time. Leave it behind, honey, look to tomorrow!"

Charlotte nodded. In her rib cage there was an ache of loneliness so sharp it felt as though her lungs couldn't find air. She sucked breath in quickly. But breath wasn't the same thing as her brother, and the loneliness was still there. They had promised not to contact each other till Halloween. They needed room, her brother said. Time. They had to be alone for a while. Because they couldn't be lame. They had to declare themselves, walk up to somebody and say, "Hey, what's happening?" And if they had each other to confide in they knew they wouldn't do it.

But that night, before she went to bed, Charlotte left a message on her dad's cell phone and had a short, worried *I'm fine, are you okay?* conversation with her mother. For privacy, she went out to the stairway. Stacey was in bed when she returned, and in the yellow glow from the Daffy Duck night light that her roommate had plugged into the outlet over her desk, Charlotte found her bed and lay down on top of it. She closed her eyes, but she couldn't sleep. The facts of her life, viewed from her cinder block room, seemed more alarming than ever. That her father had dumped her mother for one of his grad students; that after her brother took off, her mother had blown her whole savings account to attend a week-long health and human awareness retreat in the Catskills; that when she came home she drank a quart of carrot juice every day and looked for guidance in the plastic-coated Personal Inspiration Book she kept on the kitchen table. There was the fact that at four every morning Charlotte heard the front door slam shut as her mother entered the night to power-walk the required two miles before going to work. That her mother's skin was yellow from so much carotene, that her face was gaunt and tired, that all the soft and friendly places on her body, the places Charlotte had found comfort in as a child, were now tight and hard. Her mother asked Charlotte not to tell her brother about the new program, that she would wait for the right opportunity and tell him herself. But Charlotte had called her brother right away. The terror had to be shared.

Her mother could use only organic carrots. Once a week she drove to a farm market to buy in quantity. When Charlotte opened the refrigerator, nothing was visible but the green, leafy tops spilling over the shelves. There was no other food. Cooking had stopped long ago, but now nobody shopped.

So after her brother left, all pretenses were dropped. They were like girlfriends, peeing with the bathroom door open, bitching about their periods. The nights when she woke up to her mother's muffled cries down the hall, Charlotte would crawl in beside her. Her mother always turned in early while Charlotte stayed at the computer, the angry lyrics of her favorite artists slapping against steady drum-machine beats while she IM'd her friends. Before she went to bed, she tiptoed down the hall to her mother's room, and if her mother woke up, as she often did, Charlotte went to sleep there.

This sleep they shared was comfort. Female closeness was comfort too. And didn't it grant them certain privileges? Like the assumption that once again ordinary life might resume? But now, with comfort gone, who was going to stop her mother from doing something truly crazy?

Charlotte woke up the next morning panicked and sweaty. She really wanted to talk to her brother. Daylight was flat and ugly; Daffy Duck was dull. Stacey's bed was empty, and just as Charlotte was wondering if she could turn over and go back to sleep, the door opened and Stacey returned from the shower, swishing past her in a bathrobe that matched her sheet set. She deposited a plastic tote basket on her desk that contained all of her toiletry items and, with her back turned, began to get dressed.

"Charlotte," she said softly, still facing the other direction, "there's a freshman orientation meeting in fifteen minutes."

"Thanks," Charlotte mumbled. "But I've got a terrible headache. Can you make up some excuse for me? Like the heat is making me nauseous?"

"Why *sure* honey," Stacey said brightly. "And it probably *is*. That sun's so *strong* it could bleach a black beach towel white. My cousin Tilly Mae always says that right about this time in the summer. You're just not used to *August* in Georgia." Charlotte was appalled by this gushing of sympathy but kept her mouth shut. After endless rustlings, during which she feigned sleep, she finally heard the gentle clicking as the door to the hallway was closed. Then there was a scattering of faraway voices, foot-steps, the slamming of other doors, and at last the building was empty.

Silence. She walked her familiar old self down the hall to the bathroom. It was so cavernous the door echoed when it slammed behind her. She stood under the shower and then dried herself slowly in front of the huge mirror over the sinks, puddling the floor while she stared at her nakedness. *Grief helps the body recover from loss.* It could be a thesis sentence. Meaning, grief can't be rushed, and she would never do what her mother did—pay someone to dictate her life just so she could put a proper expres-sion on her face.

That day she didn't go to the orientation meeting or the small group discussions or the afternoon panel. She missed the evening barbeque and music on the lawn. Instead, she unpacked her clothes and organized her belongings. Then she walked over the grounds. Old trees, sloping fields, there was even a stream with a wooded path beside it and a slatted bridge that crossed it. She didn't get hungry until two o'clock, and then she walked into the village. At the only restaurant she saw on Main Street, she entered the air-conditioned emptiness of a summer afternoon in the deep South, sat at the counter, and ordered a grilled cheese and an iced coffee. She noticed the silver pedestal ice cream dishes and ordered a scoop of vanilla, because she remembered sitting at a counter like that a long time ago in the North, eating ice cream out of those very same dishes with her father. Now, holding her spoon, looking for flecks of vanilla bean, she felt pathetic.

Outside again, the sun was as intense and bright as it had been earlier. It seemed that in Georgia there was no diminishing of light or heat as the day went on. Down the street she passed a garage, and the dark bays where cars were up on lifts looked cool and inviting. A group of kids, all about her age, were standing in the entrance drinking sodas.

"A hundred miles an hour!" she heard one of them say. "Believe you me. An awesome two eighty! Six thousand rpm!"

It amazed her that after only twenty-four hours their drawl had started to sound ordinary.

"Hey, what's happening?" She said it out loud and walked toward them. But as she entered the shadows of the garage, sunlight blinded her so all she saw were shapes. Still, she knew they were taking in her wild hair, the halter top with her nipples showing, her long white legs ending in the kind of clunky leather sandals she'd noticed already that girls in the South didn't wear.

There were three of them, two guys and one woman. They were too shy to answer her question and too unsophisticated to do anything but ignore her. Probably they hated the college kids and could tell that was what she was. When the man stepped out her eyes had adjusted. His face was the color and texture of old leather, his body was slim and muscled, and his hair was as grey as a winter day in New York State. He threw down his cigarette, rubbed it out with the toe of his boot, and looked over her head. "Want to see it?" he asked, sending his glance, at the very last minute, down to her.

She followed him out to the dusty parking lot and around to the back, where there were weeds growing up through the concrete and insects plunking, rubbing, and hammering at all of their insect keyboards. There was nothing else back there but a car under a blue sheet. He pulled it off and whispered, "This baby goes a hundred easy. Real easy." He drew *easy* out so long she wondered if he were making fun. "Cause that's all she was made to do. These lines, see, and the fact that her belly's slung low. Wind engineering. She tunnels through."

What kind of car it was, Charlotte had no idea, but she tried to look interested. When he unlocked the doors she peeked in and breathed the new car smell, saw all the dials on the dashboard, the plush leather seats. "It's beautiful," she said, meaning not only the car, but the sounds, the weedy parking lot, and the smell of grease on his blackened clothes.

He closed the door, hitched his pants up, ran a grimy hand through his hair. "You're not from 'round here. Passin' through or gonna stay awhile?"

"I just moved here."

"I figured that."

"I guess it shows."

"Well, let me put it this way." He flashed her a conspiratorial wink. "I take one look at you and it all comes back. Yup, every single last bit of the time when I was your age 'bout and I decided to try up North." He paused to make sure she looked surprised. "Yup, up North, Chicago. Wouldn't believe that, would you? Well I was a stubborn son of a gun. Wouldn't hear nothing from nobody, just moved on up there and found a job and after 'bout six months, yup, was six months, exactly when all the snow and ice was all stacked up and the wind was whipping your skin raw. Why one day I just said to myself, Buddy, who you kidding? Come on, this ain't where you belong and that was all I needed. I got in my car and drove on back here and I've been here ever since. It's a good place if it's right for you and if it ain't, why you'll leave and go someplace else. Meanwhile, friends are good to have, cause 'round here everybody knows everybody. Unless you're up at the college and even if you are, friends in town, well that's not a bad thing."

"I'm not at the college," she whispered.

He was walking into the shade against the building, motioning her to come along. Putting one hand on the wall beside her, he pulled a handkerchief out of his pocket to wipe his forehead. His hands were beautiful, the fingers long and straight, and his skin was bronzed as if he worked long hours outdoors.

But he was old. Thirty-five, forty. Yet the way he looked at her made her feel like maybe she wasn't the only refugee. Like maybe he knew her same troubles. Like maybe he had nothing to protect because someone, along the way, had already stolen it. And that's the way she was too. Somebody had stolen everything. Her father. She heard Stacey's words. *Leave it behind, honey, look to tomorrow. Not yet,* she whispered inside. *Not yet.*

Her arm was covered with goosebumps. Her teeth were chattering. It was fear of some sort, a physical reaction she couldn't control, and in that hundred-degree heat it was embarrassing. The same thing had happened when her father parked a U-Haul in front of their house and they helped him to carry out his desk, his computer, his bookshelves. Maybe it happened because she was thin.

All around them the keyboardists were banging away in the long grass. She noticed that in the manner he was standing, his arm and his body closed her in. What made him so presumptuous? She might have cried out like the girl in the song, *You disrespectin me?* and he might have answered like the guy, *I'm not fukin wichu.* But he was. That's what was happening in those minutes they didn't speak. He'd figured out she was a virgin.

"Ed Fisk. But you wouldn't want to shake my hand cause you wouldn't believe the monster engine I just pulled. I am black grease from head to feet." He showed her his elbow, but she looked at the grease on his face and the flecks of yellow in his green eyes. Not Stacey's yellow. An ancient yellow, close to gold. Maybe he drank carrot juice too. "You got some time, sister? A couple of hours for an old sinner like me, seeing as how we both know what it's like to be lonesome?"

"Sure," she said timidly, arms crossed over her chest.

"Well, let me just put my tools away, close up shop, and then I'll take you for a spin in this miracle of automotive engineering."

She bought a soda from the machine in his waiting room. Then she stood with the others, who she found out later were Bud, Clive, and Mary. She hoped they weren't going to come along, and she was pretty sure they weren't, because in the slow and kind of zombie-like fashion of kids who had nowhere to go and nothing to do, which was just like she and her brother had been in *their* small town, they seemed to be getting ready to move on.

The cold drink intensified her chill. But she kept sipping, because it gave her something to do. It amazed her how patient everyone was, how they were content just to stand there in the boredom and heat. At least the other kids lacked the social skills to try and include her in their talk, which consisted of sentences like, "That Alabama girl's a ho," "She wasted to the extreme," "I mean shit-faced."

Ed was in the rear, cleaning stuff off with rags. On the street, cars went back and forth, slowing for the light in front of the restaurant and then speeding up. After what felt like an hour, he walked out and pulled the door down on the first bay. They watched from where they were standing in the second bay, but no one moved until the last minute. Then Mary, Clive, and Bud shouted "see ya!" and wandered off without even waving goodbye to Charlotte.

"Tomorrow!" Ed called, about to pull the last garage door down, but they didn't hear him, because on the sidewalk they were convulsed in fits of laughter. It was over her, Charlotte

114

knew. Mary had said something offensive. It was about the way she talked, her stringy hair, her small breasts, her funny san-dals—anything could have set them off.

Before her father moved away they had been a unit, a collection of four related people who met the world around them with the confidence and power of a united force. They had family din-ners, long conversations. They talked about things they were thinking, things that were happening, things they were reading. They asked questions. They made plans. She used to be the kind of person who wouldn't be standing here now. That's because back then this huge swirling chaos was something beyond her, a phenomenon she only observed. Safe between her parents, she felt as though adulthood were waiting. She would live in the family for a certain apprentice period, and then she would step into it, knowing exactly what to do.

But her father left before the apprentice period was over, and once he did that there was no more talking. It was a pact of si-lence which Charlotte, her brother, and her mother worked at maintaining, because what had to be said was too angry and use-less, and they were better off just keeping their mouths closed. It became the new way, like the cold cereal that passed for dinner.

As Charlotte followed Ed back to the car she knew his life was also like that, because it didn't seem to matter to him that she hadn't told him her name or why she was there. Things were, and you either took them as they were or you let them be. She was starting to see that was how most people operated. Clive, Bud, and Mary for sure. Stacey was a person from the old way, because she wanted to help, and states of being like home-sickness still meant something to her. Charlotte was beyond that. Ed and even Clive, Bud, and Mary were her people now.

She lowered herself into the passenger seat, then he got in and gunned the engine. At last the day made sense. At last the place made sense. She could see that not doing what you were supposed to do provided benefits. Danger was safety. It was the future, and it was headed in a straight line to a place she wouldn't get to any other way. There were shimmering waves up ahead, but they weren't rain or a promise of coolness, they were only a mirage which they were going to drive right through.

"When do you have to be back?" he asked as soon as they got outside of town. The big engine under the hood ticked politely, but she knew that when he gave it gas, it would take off. Catching his glance in the rearview mirror, she looked for the yellow flecks. "There's no rush," she said. She hoped he was heading for the interstate. She leaned back and closed her eyes, and when she opened them again she looked into a new distance and watched the speedometer as the car delivered them to a sensation she'd never had before. It was horizontal falling. "Just wait a bit," Ed said, foot down on the accelerator. What amazed her was the lack of noise. At a hundred, and then a hundred and ten, there were no mechanical complaints, nothing but quiet. They needed music. But there were no CDs lying around, and she had a feeling that if she turned on the radio it would not be tuned to rap or hip-hop but the self-pitying twang of country, and then she might regret everything. At that speed, the fields turned into a line. Trees fell down, cars dropped away. It didn't even occur to her to be scared. That's because the falling sensation, once you got used to it, was OK. They crossed into Alabama. Nothing was different. But when he slowed down to turn off at an exit, and pulled into the entrance for a motel, she got the chill once again. They nosed up to the office, he shut the car off, and looking out the windshield said, "This okay with you?"

With teeth chattering, she said yes, because everything had been decided already. *Inappropriate sex is not a smart way to get back at your parents*: a thesis sentence flashing in neon. But when he returned with the key, she followed him into the little room which was too warm and smelled like someone had covered the cigarette smoke with lots of pine air freshener. There were shiny gold quilts on the beds, drapes at the windows to match.

"Excuse me a moment. I need to wash up." She heard him lock the bathroom door and turn on the shower. His keys were on top of the TV, and she considered stealing them and driving away. But where would she go? Her father was right. Life was absurd. Here she was, two jets and one propeller plane away from the starting point, and she was in a motel with an old guy, a guy who liked country music.

She sat on the end of the bed and looked at her hands. She was going to stay right there. She was going to see how it would happen. Happiness was impossible to hope for and silly anyway to consider.

But when the water stopped she got nervous. There were rustlings, something fell in the tub, and then the lock was sprung. He strode out naked. She'd seen male genitals before but only a glimpse and that by accident. Of course it was rare to find a girl her age who was still a sexual novice, and sometimes that embarrassed her. She should have planned better. It probably had to do with her brother and the fact that they had all the same friends. In any case, she was what she was, so she stared. He walked over to the curtains, peeked out, turned on the air conditioning, saw her still watching him, and smiled. He had dimples. That relieved her. In fact, he looked as goofy as Stacey's Daffy Duck night light. Now he was holding himself.

"Does this strike terror? I sincerely hope not. But then maybe it do. Maybe this is your first time. In which case, sister, you're in good hands, we'll take it slow and easy cause I want it to be real nice for you, baby."

First sister, now baby. No one had ever called her these things. *Asshole*, her brother said. She called him *asswipe*. She lay back on the puffy quilt, her arms at her sides. Ed put his arms around her, and under the fragrance of soap she caught a hint of sweat. It was something wild, something that could never be predicted or understood. He kissed her on the mouth at the same time he unbuttoned her shirt, and when her breasts spilled out, she felt his head turn downward, his calloused fingers slide over her skin.

Hold on a minute, she wanted to say. Such sudden ownership. Such casual privacies. "Hold on a minute," she said out loud, pushing his head away, sitting up.

Natives and Strangers

Summer vacation swooped in with the hot weather and trapped his sorry self in the sticky web of family. No regular meals, no state requirements, nothing at all to take him away from the pile of buildings after the bend on Quigg Hollow Road where the Dear Cutter sign stood at the silver mailbox. All those very important things all those very important people made him learn, once summer arrived, had no influence.

Math and science were useless. History might have had a purpose because Sam's father was a Vietnam vet, and history might help explain some things. But once the endless days got themselves going, his mother napping through the warm afternoons, which meant she was as good as gone when his father was raging in the kitchen, explanations didn't matter. He had to get low, stay quiet, very, very quiet, quiet as the dog Sunshine when he was watching a bug, and keep to himself. Not talking, not saying anything except those times when he was asked something directly. He was no different from the animals, including the insects, the birds, but mostly the insects. He was no different, certainly no better, and that wasn't a bad thing. It got him through the summer and up to the day school began again when he could rise from insect to human and think his way into all of those problems they tossed out. Like, what is the square root of 77? In summer it didn't make any difference if it was 8.7 or minus 3. It made no difference at all.

The emptiness of the days was a fact more frightening than any others. Or maybe he just wasn't the type to have friends. That summer, besides being a bug and staying low and quiet, he did a lot of riding on his bike, miles and miles, and every day he stopped in the marsh across from the house at the end of Quigg Hollow Road to watch. First the For Sale sign had appeared. That's what caught his interest in the first place. Who would want to live on Quigg Hollow, where it was only Sperry, the deer cutter, and farther down, a bunch of hardly used hunting camps? But the previous fall somebody had built the house on the stretch of brushy land just off of 417, and then on June first, the For Sale sign appeared.

"Goddammit to Hell," his father stormed. "Now they speculatin'! Just like in them cities! And if that house sells, they gonna build another. Then another, and next thing you know, taxes'll hit the ceiling."

After the For Sale sign, there were visits by the realtor, then the Sold sign, and then, in July, a moving truck.

On the Saturday the moving truck came, Sam had hidden his bike in the marsh across from the house where he had been watching all summer long. He was standing at his usual post behind the black willow when a white car pulled into the driveway. A tall, thin man stepped out and walked over to the truck. Sam could hear him talking, laughing. Then two men got out of the truck and joined the thin man on the driveway. They all looked toward the house, a two-story house with a two-car garage. As the men unloaded the truck, the thin man checked each piece of furniture. There was some conversation over a sofa. Raised voices over a bookcase. Nothing was said about the bicycle. It was the first hint Sam had that there was a boy in the family. He hardly noticed the belongings that came after it, or the tricycle. His eyes were on the bicycle the father had parked in the sun next to the garage.

It was a mountain bike. It looked to be brand-new, and its shiny black tires, even at rest, had all the traction country travel required. They'd carry a boy up to the top of the hills, spin him down through the valleys, and out along the endless dirt roads that went to no place, and then even beyond no place into the miles of state forest land. It might have had twenty gears by the look of it, and right away he hated the boy that was going to live there.

Maybe it was that hatred that made him such a diligent spy. That summer when he crouched in the soft mud under the willow, Sam made himself secret. He knew how to slip from shadow to shadow, fitting his body into the shapes that were already there, or if the space was empty, getting low to the ground and fast like a fox. It was how he moved at his own house, avoiding his mother's spells, his father's anger. But the most important thing he knew how to do was watch. He knew that a person who was being watched always felt it, so he'd learned, over the years, how to watch without watching, how to listen without appearing to listen.

Sam was in his regular hiding place on the day the tall, thin man arrived with his family. He saw the little girl tumble out of the van and run onto the porch. She was a blur of frills and ribbons, a fluffy summer dress and curly hair that bounced in the sunlight. She clapped her hands in excitement, called out in her high, little girl voice and her very prettiness and excessive gladness made him hate the boy even more. Emerging more slowly from the van, he looked to be the same age as Sam, and after the happy sister, his stillness was strange. He stood in the driveway not moving, just looking around. The first place his gaze went was the willow across the road. Something made the boy's glance stop right there. When he had an entire house with a front porch, a back deck, and a side yard with swings, when his brand-new mountain bike gleamed against the wall of the garage, his eyes stayed on the willow. Sam didn't worry; he knew he couldn't be seen. He had pressed himself into the tree and was looking without appearing to look, and the spot was so familiar to him by that time and his clothes so dirty and washed out, he had melted into the general colors. The boy's father came over, put his arm on the boy's shoulder, and turned him back to the house.

But Sam still felt the effect of that gaze. The steady eyes, the tousled blond hair, the rumpled clothes made a gash in the afternoon, and it was some time before it felt safe enough to crawl over to his bicycle, push it through the tangled growth, and ride back to his place.

—⟡—

Nelson Sperry was known in all the surrounding towns because his was the only deer cutting business that hadn't been shut down by county health. During hunting season, from mid November to mid December, there was a steady stream of pickups hauling dead animals to the Sperry place. The business was in the barn. There was a room with long plastic-wrapped tables, a couple of sinks, and a wall of old refrigerators. It was painted white and at all times during the season kept scrupulously clean, a necessity in case an inspector showed up, and an effect of Agatha Sperry's control over the one small area of life she could claim. Nelson had built the room inside the dark, cavernous space of the barn where deer carcasses were sometimes piled eight deep on the floor. The Sperrys worked day and night during the season in order to keep up, neither one of them sleeping more than four hours. January and February were the months they recouped from their November and December labor. Agatha usually got sick, Nelson went on a binge, and things generally fell apart until the next October, when the room had to be scrubbed down and painted, fresh plastic wrapped around the tables, knives sharpened, packing supplies ordered, and the grinder taken apart and cleaned.

Agatha followed the health codes meticulously, and by October her conversation had frequent references to "that son of a bitch from the county." She told Sam the inspector would drive an unmarked car, and it would be a new car, but with no chrome. "You watch for it, Sammy, let me know. Any car like that driving slow on this road. You come on in here and tell me."

Her brown hair, stiff and lifeless from too many home treatments, stood up around her head in clumps, and her body, which had long ago succumbed to the twin ravages of Sammy's birth and marriage's disappointments, bulged underneath her clothing in places not normally associated with the contours of a woman's body. Her thighs were heavy but her buttocks flat. Her breasts were collapsed, but her waist was a thick roll.

"You watch for me now, won't you? Don't wait for Sunshine to bark. Cause Sunshine, he practiculy blind these days, ain't you sweetheart?" The old hunting dog turned his milky eyes in her direction. An encounter with a raccoon many years ago had left his face with a perpetually surprised expression. One chewed ear flopped down, the other stood up at attention.

Agatha scooped Sam into her body and squeezed him mightily. "You my good boy," she said in the same tone she'd used with the dog. "You my best sweetheart. Now bike on into town will you and buy us something for supper." She pulled a wad of bills out of her pants pocket and counted out ten ones, which she placed in his hands. "Coffee too. Don't forget."

Back then, no one lived at the house on the corner where Quigg Hollow Road junctioned with 417. So once Sam had pumped up his tires, he could run to the market and back without speculations about anyone. But by July, all that had changed. He could never just ride past that house anymore. He always hid in the marsh for a while. That was how, a week after they'd moved in, he discovered the boy's name. Not that it mattered. He wasn't interested in the boy so much as the bike. Fact is, he'd spent so much time over there every day watching it, he was starting to feel like the bike was his. And not only that. The boy didn't ride it. No one had touched it since the day the father had first wheeled it over. How could you have a bike like that and not ride it? Sam decided that the object of his hatred, the boy with the steady eyes and the long look, had to be really stupid. Which made sense maybe in alphabetic logic, because his last name began with the same letter: Sims. That was the name painted in white paint on the side of the black mailbox. He did wonder if the boy had a different name, but he decided that if that were so, it would have been painted on the mailbox too.

Sims' mother looked like the kind who got married and divorced all the time, so there might have been a different father. She was where the blond hair came from, and since the little girl was dark like the man, that might have been the situation. Which was another reason to hate him. His own mother's scorn for the families they saw in the Kmart, where women with figures and attractive looks pushed carts loaded with kids and toys and items nobody really needed, was his scorn too, without his having made a decision about it. So when the boy's mother came out on the porch one evening in all white, a white shirt and white pants, he heard his mother's caution about any woman who got herself up in sexy clothes: "That lady's got boyfriend on the brain. Trust me, she'll be divorced soon enough." Sims' mother put her hand over her eyes and scanned the area around the house. Seeing nothing she called, "Jasper!" The little girl came to stand beside her. "Jasper!" the little girl called. Then the mother lifted the girl into her arms and they called together, "Jasper, dinner!"

So that was his name. Watching from the tree, Sam felt the same kind of dislocation he'd get when he was watching a movie. The pretty house with the pretty mother and the pretty little girl felt like it was part of a story. And he was right there watching it, close as could be, and yet it would never be his. As soon as the door shut behind them, Sam rolled onto the ground and lay there, face down, breathing. That was better. The heat from the afternoon had collected in the soft, powdery dirt and its warmth smashed into his face and belly where his shirt rode up and he could feel ants crawling and clumps of weeds pressing into his skin. He could have stayed there till it got dark, but he heard a small noise behind him, nothing to worry about, just a bird picking for bugs, or a rabbit passing through. Still, he lifted his head to look and was surprised to see a blur of red. Jasper Sims had been wearing a red shirt yesterday, so he said slowly, like he didn't care one way or the other, "I knew you was there all long."

If his mother had taught him to be suspicious of pretty women, his father had taught him never to let anyone catch him with his pants down. "And if they do," Nelson explained, "it's best you never let them know it." "I was just waiting to see how long it was 'fore you said something. Your mommy wants you, didn't you hear?"

Still, he didn't turn to look at the boy. That's because he was hoping that maybe the boy wasn't there at all, that the flash of red had been a cardinal and not a shirt. So he spoke to the ground and kept his eyes on the soft mulch underneath him. But it didn't work. Because after a moment filled with the buzzing of a mosquito, a voice came out of the brush behind him. "And do you know how long I've known you've been here?"

It was a quick, eager voice. It wasn't afraid of making mistakes or being laughed at; it was a voice that was sure of itself. "Yeah?" he said, keeping his head down, because he didn't care at all and he already knew what the boy looked like, "how long?"

"Since yesterday. That's when I knew for sure. But I've been suspecting it for longer than that."

"Well your mommy wants you to supper, so you better run on in and do what she says."

"She can go fuck herself," the voice said in such a level, serious tone that Sam laughed, forgetting this was his enemy.

Jasper took that as an invitation. He crept out of his hiding place and said, "You live down the road. Deer Cutters. What grade are you going into this fall?"

Sam was sitting up now. He was facing Jasper, who was still a ways off, half in, half out of a stand of milkweed, still too far away to notice Sam's embarrassment. Since fourth grade, which was the grade they'd made him do twice, he'd had the worry that he was dumber than anyone else. That's why he said, "None your business."

"Well, then, how old are you?"

"Thirteen."

"Good. I'm thirteen too. And I'm going to be the best friend you ever had in your whole life."

"Say what?" Sam cried. It was an expression his father used when he was opening the mail and a bill appeared. Then he'd sputter, "Don't think so!" and throw the bill into the trash. That was how the Sperry compound came to have no telephone and electricity only in the winter months, when money from deer cutting filled the silverware drawer in the kitchen.

"Best friends," Jasper repeated.

The purple wash of the coming evening had made his eyes go violet. His hair was so blond it looked white, and his skinny legs, poking sockless from under pants that were much too clean, were pale. He was nothing but a city boy with an expensive bicycle he never even rode. "Not if I can help it," Sam said and stood up, slowly brushing the dirt and leaves off his jeans. He walked deeper into the muck, lifted his bike, pushed it out to the road, and went off on low tires. The freezing and thawing of too many winters had cracked the rubber, and there were slow leaks in each one. Though he pumped them full of air every morning, by every late afternoon they were down again. But low tires made tricks easy. So he hoped Jasper was watching, because he lifted the front wheel up off the road and pedaled forward on the back, balanced perfectly until he got to the curve.

Every Monday evening Nelson Sperry played at the Hootenanny. Sam and Agatha rode along with him, and in the recreation room at the Lutheran Church, where everyone in the town who could sing or play an instrument gathered once a week to entertain each other, they occupied two of the folding metal chairs in the audience. The performers sat in a semicircle at the front of the room. Most played acoustic guitar, a couple played electric, one person played banjo, and two people played fiddle. All of them sang, but no one sang as well as Nelson. Nelson didn't play an instrument at all. But there was so much melody in his voice alone, an instrument wasn't necessary. Nelson was also the only one who sang the kinds of songs Frank Sinatra had made popular. The others played country songs, and the audience, which was old people mostly, got up to do the two step, husbands with wives, women with women, and unpaired romantic hopefuls.

When Nelson sang, no one danced. That was not only because he wasn't playing an instrument, but also because a man like Nelson having a voice like that, a voice you could hear in New York City if you paid a lot of money and went to a fancy Broadway play, was a miracle. Out of respect, they sat through Nelson's numbers. And in a way nobody could have explained, the miracle touched Agatha and Sam too, who of course lived with Nelson, day in, day out, and most of the time found him to be no miracle at all.

Nelson was always in the first position. That meant he was the one to open the evening, and since everyone performed twice, he was also the one to close it. He only knew about a dozen tunes all the way through and didn't often bother to learn new ones. Still, he belted the familiar ones out so sweet and perfect, the audience gave him long applause. Nor did any other performer get the amount of catcalls and whoops and whistles that he did. He was their star, the reason the Monday Hootenanny had been started and the reason everyone came.

And he gave them a good show. He looked good on Monday nights. He wore a clean pair of jeans, held up with a black leather belt instead of the old brown one he used for the pants he wore at home. The blue knit shirt, summer or winter, was unbuttoned halfway to give a glimpse of a widespread, masculine chest. He reeked of aftershave, and his long, grey hair, moussed into a casual, windblown effect, was so stiff that were he to stand near a fan, not a filament would be disturbed. He had the blotchy red face of a drinker, and the beers he consumed before the event made his cheeks glisten.

But at the Hootenanny, a lot of men had damp faces and beer guts. They stood by the refreshment table, cracking jokes, whispering nasty things about women they didn't even know. Nelson was just another one until he got up to the mike, then Sam watched his father become someone better.

On that Monday he stood up before he started and made an announcement. "I got a new song for you folks." There were titters of laughter, and he said, "Yup, I've learned me a new one for your listening pleasure." That caused more laughter. Someone cried, "Way to go, Nelson!" He smiled, gave them a salute, and went on. "And I'm gonna try it, but I'm nervous, see, I'm afraid I'm gonna forget the words. So Agatha here, she's got a nice voice too, Agatha's gonna help me. It's called, 'You're Getting to Be a Habit With Me.'"

Sam, who was seated next to Agatha, had noticed that his mother seemed more nervous than usual. Now she walked up to the front of the room, and the performer next to Nelson moved his chair over. Agatha looked terrified, but when Nelson hummed a note, she hummed it along with him, and then, with Nelson beaming at the audience, they began:

Every kiss, every hug
Seems to act just like a drug
You're getting to be a habit with me

While he was singing, Nelson danced in place, sliding two steps to one side, two steps to the other. At first, Agatha didn't know what he was doing and stood awkwardly, then she did the two steps with him, and by the second stanza their movements were in sync:

> *Let me stay in your arms*
> *I'm addicted to your charms*
> *You're getting to be a habit with me*

Then Nelson twirled her and she actually twirled. She gave a big smile, and her voice by the last stanza was strong and steady:

> *Oh, I can't break away*
> *I must have you every day*
> *As regularly as coffee or tea*

The last lines, which were high, Nelson did alone and Agatha merely swayed and hummed:

> *You've got me in your clutches and I can't break free*
> *You're getting to be a habit with me.*

For most of the song, Sam couldn't see his parents through the throng of folks that were sitting in front of him, and that was just as well, because the strange lumps of his mother's body made her into a spectacle he would rather not have to stare at. He was scared for her, but by the end, when applause filled the room and Agatha smiled broadly, he was clapping as hard as everybody else. When she walked back to her seat Nelson said,

"There she goes, folks, there goes the sweetest woman in the whole wide world." He sat back down, and Ronnie Digges went next. He was in his twenties, a town boy, a drug addict some said, and he had an electric guitar and a yodel that was a little slow and creaky, but he knew how to lead up to it good, and when to let it go. Most importantly, he strummed a good rhythm, so right away people got up to dance.

After him were Ellen and Burt Tarwater, husband and wife, who played "Walkin' at Midnight" and sang in tremulous voices. That's when Agatha leaned over and said, "How'd I do?"

"You were great, Mom," Sam whispered, and it wasn't a lie.

On the way home Agatha said, "The Singing Sperrys, Nelson, Agatha, and Sam, how 'bout it?"

"I can't sing," Sam said quickly.

"Well you're wrong on that, sweet boy, you have a beautiful voice."

Nelson, who drove with the front seat pushed back so he could slouch down and steer with the help of his knee said, "Since when have you heard it? Kid keeps his mouth locked at all times. Let's hear you on 'America the Beautiful.' Come on. I know you know the words cause you sing it at school. *Oh beautiful . . .*" he started. "Well? *For spacious skies . . .* Huh? Can I hear you? *For amber waves of grain . . .* What was that? Didn't hear you!" He turned to Agatha and said, "See? The boy might have a good voice, but he don't want to sing. Fact is, he don't want to do anything. Fact is, he's a loser. Am I right kid? Huh?" He turned around to look at Sam in the back seat. Then he said to Agatha, "I wouldn't make any plans 'round a loser like him."

"Takes one to know one," Agatha said quietly.

"What was that?"

"I said you should keep your mouth closed if you don't have nothing kind to say."

"Meaning I wouldn't say a goddammed word all week. Cause all that boy does is antagonize."

"Just do me a favor and don't talk to him. You have no 'preciation for your own flesh and blood and I'm sick to death of the whole situation. Sick to death and tired of it, hear me?"

Everyone was quiet the rest of the way home, although every once in a while Nelson would come out with a rich rendering of another line from "America the Beautiful." He'd follow that with a hearty laugh and slap the steering wheel, his rings clicking against the glittering plastic strip wrapped around it.

—❧

The pile of buildings people called the Sperry place had been created by accidental events, beginning with the original pink and grey 1957 trailer which somebody had been hauling someplace else when their truck broke down. Considering the cost of repair, they looked at the land on Quigg Hollow Road and discovered it was as good a location as where they'd been headed. So they pushed the truck to its final resting place in the back field, set the trailer in the lap of the valley, and stayed there three or four years. It was empty for several years after that, until a

young Nelson Sperry, returned from Vietnam and having diffi-
culty getting started on the plan he'd formulated for the rest of
his life, bought it for back taxes.

Now the trailer contained only the kitchen, the bath, and
Agatha's bedroom. That's where she stayed for the three days
after the Hootenanny, when rain drummed a steady staccato
beat on the metal rooftop and gave her a headache.

Nelson remained in his territory, the workshop he'd built ad-
jacent to the trailer in the years when he'd had a cabinet-making
business. Later, he'd cut a door in the kitchen and built a passageway that connected the workshop with the trailer. Now it
was his bedroom, a dark place with clothes draped over the saws
and tables. The passageway, hammered together from lumber
scraps and pieces of Plexiglas, was cold but dry.

Sam's room used to be the living room. Like the workshop, it
was a small wooden shack built next to the trailer. But from the
start, this one was built directly next door so Sam could step
down into it from the kitchen. It had two windows, a rug, and a
sofa where Sam slept. It was the most orderly space in the compound. Sam's clothes were always put away in the chest of drawers, his sleeping bag was folded on the end of the sofa, and there
was a stack of books on top of the chest that Sam read at night
when they had electricity. In this room, as in all the others, there
were kerosene lamps for the times when they didn't. And since
the refrigerator and stove ran on propane and three wood stoves
heated the three different structures, electricity wasn't essential.

Sam's bedroom had a door to the outside. The metal roof extended over it by a couple of feet, making a protected spot where

he could park his bike and where he could sit during a rain-
storm.

That's where Sam spent most of the three days. He watched
how the rain made holes in the grass and overran the hill back of
the compound. He also listened to his dad's conversation from
the kitchen. Nelson was sitting at the table, talking to Agatha,
who was in her room, lying down.

"A couple of goats!" he shouted. "Build a shed. Three sided,
that's all they need."

"Where's the hay gonna go?" Agatha called back.

"Build hay storage onto the shed. Then we got venison, we got
eggs, we got goat milk, we're all organic."

"How much?" she asked.

"Says here two kids. Don't say if they're the meat variety or the
milk variety. No price. Just a phone number."

"Oh, Nelson," she cried in a despairing voice, "what we gonna
do with goat milk?"

"Drink it, woman! That's where your headaches come from.
Them cows, they poison 'em with hormones and antibiotics and
such and you're just drinking down all them chemicals. Pure
unadulterated goat's milk, that's what you need. They're socia-
ble. But you gotta have a good fence cause they like to climb."

"Goats!" Agatha said in disgust. "Just what we need."

"I'm going to get me these goats."

"Not till you build 'em enclosure and good and tight," she
sputtered. "You're making my head worst just thinking 'bout it.
And not just any old thing slapped together. Good and tight."

"I'll take down that old outhouse, use the planks."

"They're rotted!" she shouted, "rotted!"

"Not a rotted board in that. Not a one."

Next thing Sam heard was Agatha's door slammed closed and Nelson muttering, "Goddammned woman, lives in the country but sees a problem with goats. Sam!"

Sam didn't get up right away. He and Sunshine were watching bugs. Sunshine was eating them. Sam stroked her one floppy ear and waited for his father to call again. Only then did he walk to the doorway of the kitchen and look at the table cluttered with dirty dishes, a can of yeast flakes, a couple boxes of cereal, a jar of instant coffee, the paper floating over it all like a cloud.

"Go get me the mail, will you, son?"

"It's pouring."

"A little wet gonna hurt you?" Nelson sipped his coffee, put the cup down and looked at him.

"It's pouring. I'll get it later when it stops."

"Is it my imagination or didn't I ask you to get the mail?"

Sam waited for his mother to come to his rescue, but there wasn't a sound from the other room. "It's only gonna be bills. What you want them for?"

"You whining boy, you whining? A simple request and you can't do it?" Now Nelson put down his cup and started to get to his feet. Sam squawked quickly, "I'll get it, I'll get it," and left.

Since he was already soaked from the short run to the mailbox, he stood in the downpour and watched how the water hit the road in bursts of white light. They flattened into wavelets and spilled into the ditch where everything bubbled and frothed, as a fast, sudden river leaped with ferocious energy, taking limbs and trash along with it. Sam stepped down into the ditch and the mad, crazy water slapped against his legs. He looked toward the curve, because something had caught his eye. There was a tall white shape coming through the sheet of rain. He watched as it assembled itself into a bike, the silver wheels spinning water through the spokes, and flickering past trees. The water sluiced off the tires, and fanned into the wavelets already there on the road. It was a ship with wheels, churning, coming closer, glittering with light as the sail, which, he could see now, was really a big hooded plastic cape hanging over the sides, held darkness.

"Hey!"

Sam didn't answer. His father was waiting for the mail and already he'd been gone too long. But he stayed where he was, feet in the gully, because deep in the darkness of the hood, a pair of eyes looked out.

"Come over to my house," the creature said.

"Can't. Doing something for my dad. Anyways, I don't know you."

But that didn't seem to make a difference. As the voice continued in a loud, excited tone, the hood slipped back, revealing messy blond hair and pale cheeks. "I'm the only one home and I want to show you something. And you have to come now because they'll be back soon."

Sam saw the droplets of water hanging off the boy's eyelashes. He was barefoot too, but that wasn't the thing that convinced him. What convinced him flashed across his vision for only a second. Jasper smiled, and Sam saw that his teeth were straight, and they were a white as dazzling as the water that shot out from the spokes of his wheels. Jasper was already lifting the back of his cape and, feeling as though he were ducking into a world of dreams, Sam slipped inside it and sat down on the seat.

When Jasper pushed off, he was jerked forward. That made it easy to put his arms around the other boy's waist. He rode blind, in the dark cave of plastic, feeling the rib cage under his hands.

"What did you want to show me?" Sam said when they ran up to the porch.

Jasper shucked the cape off and left it in a pile. Then he opened the front door and went inside. Sam followed Jasper's wet prints on the carpet and entered the stillness of the house. "You're sure this is all right?" he asked. But the way Jasper crossed the room, his hand running along the top of each piece of furniture they passed, Sam could tell that this forbidden place was ordinary for Jasper. And because he moved so freely, Sam knew it was a different kind of home Jasper had.

"This way," he said, and ran up the steps, two at a time. Sam followed more slowly. The steps were carpeted too, and now that his feet were dry, his toes sank into a softness he knew was related to wealth, luck, education. Jasper ducked into the bedroom at the far end and called, "Hurry up!" so Sam walked down the hallway past two other doors and entered the light-filled room where Jasper had disappeared. There was an enormous bed in the center of it and a jumble of plants in front of a wall of windows. Jasper was opening the drawers in a small table and dumping the contents onto the bed. Sam didn't pay any attention. He saw gleaming tile peeking through another door and went toward it, because the urge to piss was sudden and desperate. The bathroom was almost as big as the bedroom. There was a deep square tub, two sinks, and a long mirror over them that he was careful not to look into, because he knew he wasn't supposed to be there.

So it was his back the mirror reflected, a ripped shirt hanging off of wide shoulders, a tanned neck and brown wavy hair. He pissed long and loudly in the toilet. That helped him relax.

"You have to see this!" Jasper called. By the time Sam came back, there were piles of things on the bedspread. All the little foil packages were in one area, the long white tubes in another, and a flat plastic container was all by itself.

"Know what this is?" Jasper asked, picking up the container and making the lid spring open to reveal a tan rubber disk sitting inside it. "She puts it on her tits and it keeps the milk from spurting in his mouth when he sucks her."

"Yeah, sure," Sam said.

"And this," Jasper said, picking up a foil packet. "You know what this is, don't you?"

"Everyone knows what that is," Sam said.

"Here." Jasper dropped a couple in his hand. "Put them in your pocket. Just in case." He slipped a couple into his pocket too. "And now what we're going to do," he said, and he carried the rubber disk into the bathroom and started opening drawers.

"What?" Sam asked, following him, staying away from the mirror.

"Razor blade. They're around here somewhere." He flicked a switch and a dozen bulbs burst into brilliant yellow, giving the room and Jasper's skin a warm, friendly glow. Sam came closer. "Why don't you take a blade out of a razor?"

"Good idea. Hold it up into the light." He handed the rubber thing to Sam, but Sam kept his arms at his sides. "I don't want to touch it. It's your mother." So Jasper held the disk over a bulb and with a corner of the razor made a tiny slit. "That'll do. That's all we need."

"Do what?"

Jasper smiled, his teeth flashing in the mirror.

"Fix him good. When he sucks her, her milk's going to come gushing into his mouth. Babies' milk. It's disgusting."

Before they left, Jasper was very careful to put everything back exactly the way they'd found it. Then he took Sam into the kitchen and opened the refrigerator. "I'm hungry. What about you?"

But when Sam peered behind him, there was such a clutter of food staring back, the refrigerator seemed as complicated as a supermarket.

"How 'bout a sandwich? Ham and cheese? You like ham and cheese? You like mustard or mayonnaise?" Jasper put a lot of things onto the counter and Sam stood by helplessly until Jasper said, "Go ahead, we'll each make our own. Here's lettuce. Here's tomato. Here's bread."

Sam copied the other boy and made the biggest sandwich he'd ever had. "You're allowed to do this? No one's saving it for dinner?"

"No way. This is lunch stuff. Go ahead, take as much as you want."

They had ice cream after that and chocolate milk. Jasper said, "What do you want to do now?" and Sam said, "Those tubes, what were they?"

140

"That's sperm killer. The lady squirts it in her pussy in case the rubber breaks."

"Oh," Sam said, not really understanding, because he didn't know sperm was the same thing as cum.

"Ever seen one?" Jasper asked softly.

Right away, Sam's neck felt hot. He dropped his eyes to his sandwich as a picture rolled into his mind. One night early in the summer he'd heard a clatter in the kitchen followed by low, animal whining, and thinking it was the raccoon finally return-ing to finish off Sunshine, he tiptoed to the door with his flash-light, ready to flick it on and scare him away. But what his flashlight caught wasn't a raccoon at all but his mother, down on the floor like a dog, her boobs swinging loose, and his father, on his knees behind her. She reared up, screeching, and that's when he saw it, the patch of fur below her belly.

"Whose?" Jasper asked. "Whose pussy did you see?"

"Don't remember the name."

"You didn't see one, that's a lie!"

"No it ain't! I see 'em all the time. Every day!"

"Whose?" Jasper asked suspiciously.

"Your mom's."

"Well, I've seen your mom's too and let me tell you, it's a place you'd never want to go into."

When Jasper rode Sam back to his house it was still raining, so Sam took cover again under the cape. He breathed onto the warm shoulders of the boy he clasped and watched the bit of road he could see at the bottom. Before Jasper said, "Here you are, home sweet home," he saw the post holding the Deer Cutter sign and remembered his father. He retrieved the mail from the mailbox and was about to run into the house when Jasper said, "You glad you came?"

Sam didn't know how to answer. So he darted for the overhang, and when he got to it, he turned around and waved.

"See you tomorrow?" Jasper called.

"Maybe," he shouted back.

That was the start. And in the first delirious weeks of their friendship, Sam had a feeling that things were going to change. It seemed as though goodness had come down from the very sky, which, after those first days of heavy rain, was mostly blue that summer and equally flat and still over the whole county. It had to have come from the sky, because it couldn't have come from him. What did he know? What had he done to deserve it? It was sky, or maybe it was God, though he'd take sky any day because he knew sky. It was right there, close and far at the same moment. Or maybe it came from Jasper.

"You glad you came?" That was what he always asked, and Sam never once answered the question. Not because he wasn't glad, but because he didn't understand why it was necessary to say so. Jasper's family favored questions like that. The times he'd been invited for dinner, Jasper's mom would try to coax him into conversation. She wanted to know where his parents grew up, if he had any brothers and sisters.

"Your parents must like it here if they stayed on," she said. That confused Sam. Of course they'd stayed on. Where else could they have gone?

When she said, "And your father, what does he do?" and he

142

replied, "Deer cutter, ma'am," she looked startled. He watched her push the blond hair away from her face, saw the thin gold band of her wristwatch, the wedding ring on her finger. He noticed that her nails were shaped. They shone in the light. Same way her lips did. Her lipstick wasn't the kind his mother wore, which was bright red and smeary. Mrs. Sims' lipstick glistened softly. And it didn't wear off the way his mother's did, which was a relief, because on Agatha, loud red lips against her loose, washed-out skin, her dusty hair was all wrong.

"Oh, I get it," she said finally. "For hunters. Your dad butchers the deer."

"That's what he does," Sam said, though he wasn't sure that butchers was the right word. "He dresses them. Hunting season he does probably two, three thousand animals."

"You must help him then."

"Little," Sam said, the heat rising into his neck, because the truth was that during hunting season the only thing Nelson let him do was drag the carcasses out to the bucket so he could unload them into the pit. Only grunt work, when Sam had been driving the tractor and working the bucket himself since he was twelve.

"Teaches you a lot about anatomy," she said.

"Guess so," Sam agreed, though when the deer came in they were already gutted. But he'd seen the heart, the liver. Agatha cooked them up and fed them to the dog, although Nelson always bellowed, "You the one should be eating them, not Sunshine! Would cure them headaches, woman. Give ya the get up and go."

Now Sam ventured with, "Ate the innards once. Strong tasting." It was a lie, and he didn't know why he said it. The clean bright kitchen, the pretty woman asking him questions, the other boy sitting across from him at the table and always wanting to know if he was glad they were friends; it made for a kind of pressure. He felt it in his shoulders, an awkward, slippery weight that caused him to say things that weren't true and exaggerate the things that were.

"Is that why your teeth are funny?" Emily asked, plopping the top half of her body onto the table and peering into his mouth.

"Emily, what did I tell you about putting your elbows on the table? And it's rude to make a comment about someone's very nice teeth. I'm sorry, Sam, kids always say the weirdest things."

"But there's a bunch of them behind the others," she whined.

"Oh that," Sam said. "I gotta go to the dentist." He felt one of Nelson's Monday night smiles stretch his lips, but on him it wasn't convincing. He knew he wouldn't be sitting in a dentist chair anytime soon.

"Three thousand?" Jasper asked when they were walking back down the road to his house.

"Maybe not," Sam said. "Maybe it's two thousand."

"What does he charge?"

"Thirty-five bucks per animal."

They came in sight of the Sperry compound, the barn up on the rise, the trailer with its attached buildings, and coming up to them like that, after so many hours at Jasper's house, Sam saw them differently. Nothing looked solid or well-built. Not even the cars, the pickup out by the barn, the Pontiac in the driveway.

All of it seemed sunk to the ground and tilted one way or another, as though many strong winds from altogether different directions had come to that particular spot on the road and leaned against the straight lines, making every single one of them crooked.

"My dad sings," Sam said, "and he's going to get goats."

"My dad won't let us have any animals. He's allergic."

"That why your house's so clean?"

"My mom says we don't need pets. We have the birds."

"What birds?"

"The birds outside. She gave me a bird book and binoculars and you've seen those feeders out back."

Sam had never noticed. "My dad has binoculars. Not for birds though, for deer."

"Is he using them now?" Jasper asked.

"Don't think so. They're for hunting season."

"That's good," Jasper said. "Because we're going to need them."

Someone else might have asked why, but it never occurred to Sam, because in his experience things came about whether you knew why or not. And he did know why anyway. In a friendship that began with secrets dumped from a drawer onto a bed, binoculars were the obvious next step, and with September just around the bend, there was only so much time left.

But then everything stopped, because Jasper's family went on vacation. Sam tried not to miss him; he tried to return the house to the way it had first looked to him, when he felt nothing but scorn for the people who had moved in. But he couldn't get it to go back. The blankness was gone. The porch was not just a porch anymore, but the place he stood, waiting to be admitted.

The garage was not the empty building that contained a wonderful bike. It was his place now. It held three metal barrels of different kinds of bird seed, and every morning he took the lids off and filled the feeders. Mrs. Sims was paying him three dollars a day to do that.

"If you stand still and hold out the sunflower seeds," she told him, "the chickadees will pick them off your hand." Usually he was running an errand for Agatha and didn't have time to stay still for very long, but one day he stood like an idiot with a handful of seeds and he didn't move for the longest time. Nothing happened.

She don't know what she's talking 'bout, he thought. She's just a dumb, stuck-up city girl.

"Them people you know down at the end of the road?" Agatha had called out to him from her bedroom, "what's their name?"

"Sims," he said.

"Yeah. Them's the people from Buffalo. Man works at the university. Wife does too. That's two jobs they take away from locals. They don't belong in a place like this. And that boy, what's his name?"

"Jasper."

"Well, don't you bring him here. We got different ways. We don't need no snoops. You remember that so I don't have to tell you 'gen."

But Sam had never brought a friend to their house. In fact, he couldn't remember when anyone other than his mother's sister had been inside.

She called out again, her voice changed, repentant. "It's good you have a friend, Sam. It's real good."

And there he was, standing in the yard behind the Sims' house, holding out a handful of sunflower seeds because some city person who had all kinds of stupid ideas 'bout life in the country had said that if you didn't move, the chickadees would eat out of your hand. Five minutes was all the time he had to give it that day, but the next day he gave it longer, and just when he was going to give up, he heard tiny wingbeats and watched a small black and white bird swoop through the air. It settled on the feeder and cocked its head at him, its black pinpoint eyes glistening from the solid black cap on his head. Then it zipped away, dipped over his hand, and landed on the feeder again. Sam stayed still. But he didn't have long to wait, because soon, the air was filled with that tiniest of sounds, the wingbeats, and he saw the zig-zag ripple of its path. It was coming closer. It rose up an invisible column of air and zipped down it, and Sam got the feeling that maybe it was teasing him. So he stopped wanting it to come, stopped caring about the whole business. He heard his father laugh, talking to his mother. *Them people down at the end of the road, they got one of them three thousand dollar lawn tractors, brand new . . .* His feet were damp and the insides of his sneakers were damp, and then he felt the hot morning sun on his back where his tee shirt was ripped. The wingbeats came closer. They were no louder than his breath. Now he watched it the way he watched deer cross a far-off field, the tall brown shapes, full of wildness, stepping through the mess of green. All at once, the masked bird zoomed down, quickly picked a seed off his hand, zipped away, cracked it open against a branch.

After that, he stopped there twice a day. Now the chickadees swooped down straight off, grabbed a seed from his hand, and flew away. One stood on his palm once, its tiny feet tickling his skin as it looked at him, turning its head first one way and then the other.

She paid him twenty-five dollars for doing that. He stashed the money under his socks in his top drawer, with the other money he'd earned from shoveling an old lady's driveway in the winter. There was fifty now, and he figured he needed two hundred to get his teeth fixed.

Jasper was still on vacation the morning Sam woke up to a diesel motor chugging outside his bedroom. He opened his door to a strange sight: a huge container truck was backing onto their lawn, and Nelson was directing it to a place between the house and the barn. "Right there! That's good!"

A short, burly man opened the door of the cab and jumped down. He took off his cap, combed his hair back with his fingers, and appeared to study the spot where the container was going. Then he put his cap back on and said, "Looks a mite wet to me."

Nelson shook his head. "Nope, there's two ton gravel right on that spot. Had it dumped last summer. Drains good."

The man pointed above it. "My worry would be the hill. Water coming off it every storm. I estimate it run to right here, and cause it's a dip, it'll settle right here. Gravel or no."

"Nah!" Nelson waved that idea away. "I'll build a ditch if that's a problem."

The other man toed the earth, looking for the gravel, but it seemed as though all his boot dug up was clay. "My judgment, and I been in this business twenty-three years, you're asking for trouble."

"Well, that's the right place. It's convenient. When there's two foot snow, hell, you don't want to have far to walk. Besides, that trailer, if it rots through, I'll just get me another."

The container was white corrugated metal with big red letters on both sides spelling out *Wavely*.

"Right true," the man agreed. He stood on his bowed legs, doubt perched on his forehead, looking around the property. Then he climbed back into the cab. There were mechanical sounds. He hopped out again and went behind the cab, where he seemed to be busy with levers. Then, back in his seat, there was a low whine. Suddenly, the truck bed tilted upward till the backside of the container hit the ground. There was a mechanical squeal and it was pushed down along the deck and onto earth. "All right then?" he asked, leaning out of the cab and catching Nelson's thumbs-up in the mirror, he pulled the truck forward till the container was off it completely. Then he lowered the deck and drove the empty flatbed onto the road. With a wave, he was gone.

That was when Sam came forward. The container was almost as long as the trailer they lived in. It was ugly and industrial. "What's this for?"

"This here's gonna be our new barn. It's for the goats, boy. They're coming soon and you and me gonna build a wall inside this to separate the hay loft from the animal pen. Then we gonna cut a doorway into the back part for the hay. See how nice it gonna be?" Nelson pulled one of the doors open in the front and Sam saw the metal floor, the long, dark interior.

But not with his own eyes. He saw it through the Sims' eyes, and the long, misplaced container that was already sunken into their earth, swallowed in their weeds, made no sense. "Why don't we just put up a shed? Outta planks?"

Nelson ignored him. "Yes sir, my boy, it's time you learned some carpentry skills. Before the goats come, we got some work to do."

"Wavely," Agatha muttered later in the kitchen. "What the hell is Wavely?"

"Haven't the foggiest, and I don't see what it matter."

"It matter because it's right out there in full view to the whole road! And while I'm at it, did you ever consider discussing it with me before you went and paid good money for that piece of junk?"

"Whose goats is it?" Nelson bellowed from the stove where he was heating yesterday's coffee in a saucepan. "Whose the one gonna be milking and doin' ever single last thing cause you sure couldn't be bothered and the boy here, he don't care."

"Don't you bring him into this."

"That's what I'm saying! It come down to me!" Nelson shouted. "Always down to me! So if I want Wavely for my goats, Wavely is what they gonna have!"

"Suit yourself. But I'll tell you why it come down to you. Nastiness, Nelson. Who you think wants to be around when you such a mean, nasty hothead, huh?"

"I ain't talking to you, woman."

"Huh?" She went back to her bedroom and Nelson, for his

part, began to sing in a low voice at the stove as he broke two eggs into a pan that was already sitting there with last week's venison fat in the bottom of it.

> *I've heard that lizards and frogs do it*
> *Layin' on a rock*
> *They say that roosters do it*
> *With a doodle and a cock*

"How you like my new song?" he called.
"Sounds dirty," Agatha called back.
"Just a little ditty, a sweet little ditty."

> *I'm sure sometimes on the sly you do it*
> *Maybe even you and I might do it*
> *Let's do it, let's fall in love*

⸺ ꙮ

The first day Jasper was back, they met at his mailbox early in the morning. It was still cool; the air was ribboned with odors, the too sweet smell of a dead animal, the sharp musk of a bear having rolled through. Across the road, Sam saw a doe and her fawn picking their way over the hummocks. They blended so well with the colors of the distance Jasper would never have seen them without the binoculars. But Sam's eyes were sharp from three years of hunting with his father. He knew how they moved, where they went, and what time of day they were visible.

Jasper's family didn't hunt. Somehow he knew that from the very first, without them ever saying it. Something about Mrs. Sims made him think that maybe they didn't approve of hunting. It was her extra questions and the feeling she wouldn't have asked them if her husband were there.

It was Jasper who suggested they learn to identify the birds. It would give them practice in using the binoculars. "We have to zero in on things," Jasper said. "Find the details, the mysteries."

A friend made the ordinary world more interesting. Sam still kept his basic bug nature, because it was summer, still the time of danger, but now, with Jasper's bird project, things got raised to a level closer to school. So before, what was only a bunch of birds at the feeder became song sparrows and red-wing black-birds. Knowing what they were gave him confidence.

One morning, Sam followed the slow circles a big bird made as it dipped down through the sky. Its belly was white, and when its tail feathers caught the sun they glinted red. "It's a red-tailed hawk," he said, the same bird Nelson cursed when it attacked their chickens. He knew that from way up there, hawks could see voles running through a field, so Agatha's chickens were easy prey.

"What we're going to do next," Jasper said, watching the hawk, "if you want to, that is, and I hope you do" (he flashed his white teeth at Sam), "is you're going to get your dad's binoculars and we're going to go out at night and spy on people." Right away, Sam saw Agatha in the doggie position, caught by the beam of his flashlight. And even though that was a secret he wished he didn't have, he liked the idea of discovering others. It was part of the heat, part of the dark when he lay on the couch alone in his bedroom and listened to owls and coyote and the sudden, breathy snort of deer. Everything out there stayed in one spot in the daytime, but at night, under cover of darkness, it moved. It turned to prey, it turned to predator. And which would he and Jasper be, slinking around?

The plan was to meet at Jasper's mailbox at ten. Jasper would have his binoculars and Sam was to steal his dad's. That might have been easy, but he kept them in the pickup and the door groaned so loudly every time it was opened, you could hear it in the house.

"Where's your father going?" Agatha would say. "Why don't he take the car?"

The pickup was old, but it wasn't rusted. Nelson kept it off the road in the winter, out of the salt, but from years under the sun its metal sides were dulled. It seemed solid, less a wheeled object made for travel than a small building resting in front of the barn, a phenomenon like Wavely.

Agatha herself didn't drive anymore. She had Sam to run errands to the supermarket and Nelson to pick her medicines up to the pharmacy, so year in, year out, there was never any reason for Agatha to leave. She seemed as permanent and unchanging as everything else.

That afternoon, Sam squirted 3-in-1 oil on the hinges of the pickup's door, and that night, when he pushed in the chrome button, the door swung open without complaint. Shuffling blind through the clutter on the seat, his hands soon closed around the hard plastic of the binoculars.

Jasper was already there, a black shape that detached itself from the driveway and followed Sam the three miles to the village. Sam did that ride every day, and because he knew where the bumps and potholes were, he kept a fast and steady pace.

They didn't speak until their bikes were stowed under the bridge on East Avenue. "Let's see them."

Sam handed the binoculars to Jasper, who right away, declared them too dirty to use. It was just like Nelson, Sam thought, to have a pair of binoculars a person couldn't see with. But Jasper pulled off his tee shirt, and while Sam watched, wet a corner with creek water to clean the lens. Now they'll be good," he said.

They walked into the village. "Over there." Jasper pointed, and they both looked into the lighted second-story window of the last house on the street and saw a closet door standing open. "Maybe it's a lady's bedroom."

"We don't want that lady," Sam said. An old woman lived there by herself. It was her driveway he shoveled every winter, and the only secret she had was her bad breath. They went behind her house where all the backyards of the other houses on the block connected, giving them lots of windows to look into. But the problem was dogs. One was tied up outside barking. "Roger! Stop it!" a voice called. Another barked from inside and a back door opened. "Danny? Is that you?"

They ran back to the sidewalk. "What we need to find," Jasper said, "is a house all by itself where there isn't a dog."

Sam started walking.

"What? You know a place?"

"No."

"Then, where are we going?"

It was another one of the Sims family questions. "Nowhere."

"Well, why not that street?" They'd just passed Center Street.

"There's lots of dogs down there."

"Well, I think we need a plan. We can't just wander around."

Sam stopped. "You have to be quiet because sound carries. 'Specially at night. We're just going to wander around and when we find a place without dogs, we're going to sneak to the back and check it out."

"That's a plan," Jasper said. "That's a good plan. See, that's what I mean."

"Okay, now shut up."

On every street they roused a dog until they got to Second Street where an invisible tomcat yowled into the night. The first two houses were completely dark. But the next house had a light on at the downstairs window, and when they crept around to the back, two second-story windows spilled blocks of lemony yellow onto the lawn. "Follow me," Sam whispered, and darted from one tree to another until they were opposite the windows and crouched down side by side against the barn in the back.

Jasper put the glasses up to his eyes. "Nothing so far," he reported.

Sam was looking into the downstairs window. It was someone's kitchen. He didn't know who lived there, and although the kitchen was big and had lots of counters and cupboards, it was as messy as the kitchen at his house. There were dishes piled on all of the surfaces and boxes and bottles of food. With the binoculars, he could see corn flakes, tomato sauce, Mueller's Spaghetti.

"Find anything?" Jasper asked.

"Not yet." Sam kept the glass to his eye. The clutter, he thought, was a pretty good secret just on its own.

"I see something!" Jasper whispered excitedly. "Check this out!"

Sam didn't want to leave his view, so he said, "What do you see?"

"This woman, she's sitting on the bed!"

"Yeah?"

His voice dropped to an ordinary whisper. "That's all, she's just sitting there. Wish she'd hurry up and get undressed."

A man came into the kitchen.

"I think she's talking to someone," Jasper said.

Sam saw the man go over to a doorway and stop. "She's talking to the guy down here."

"Well, she's going on and on. She's getting all worked up. She's moving her hands. Wish I could hear what she's saying."

In the kitchen, the guy threw up his arms, moved away, moved back, and appeared to say something.

"If we get closer, maybe we can hear them."

"And maybe they'll be able to see us. *You* can move closer," Sam said, "but I'm going to stay here."

Suddenly, Jasper dropped his binoculars down into Sam's territory. "Look at that place. It's like crazy people live there. Would you believe that mess?"

"Wait a minute. Look upstairs. Something's happening."

"She's only opening the closet door. She's just standing there, looking inside. Now she's closing it."

The man left the kitchen, then returned with a jacket over his arm. "I think the guy's going away."

Sam noticed the car parked in the driveway, a Pontiac just like Nelson's; it even looked about the same age. The screen door slammed, the guy came outside, and with quick sharp steps walked over to the car and opened the door. Right before the first grinding of the engine Sam hissed, "Drop down!" and just as the headlights came on, the boys dove to their bellies. The space where they'd been sitting only a moment before was lit up like a movie screen.

The lights pulled away from the garage, then swung over to the neighbor's house as the car turned onto the street.

"That was close," Jasper whispered. His face was a sickly greenish color.

"Wish you weren't here?" Sam asked. Jasper looked scared. But he didn't answer. Instead, he put the binoculars up to his eyes and said, "Hey, look at this." Sam moved his glasses up to the second story too. The woman had opened the closet again, and he could see something moving inside it. "It's just like in this detective novel I read," Jasper whispered, and they watched as the shape became a man. He looked older and far more important than the man in the kitchen, because he had a mustache and was wearing a suit. Certainly, he was more romantic, because as soon as he came into the room, he took the woman into his arms and they fell onto each other, their hands, their mouths touching everyplace. They were one creature with four arms and two heads, and then everything was blocked out for a moment by cloth. And when the cloth floated down to the floor the boys saw it was the woman's dress. Her bra went sailing through the air next. And after that, there were breasts.

Just like the ones he had seen in his own sorry brain. Up there in the night sky. The window floated in the darkness and with an awe that included not only her, but himself, that spot on the earth, that night of all nights, and the other boy, he stared. It was the conjunction of dreams and reality, and he could feel how this vision was going to cure him of the other one. Because ever since he'd been unfortunate enough to glimpse his mother's heavy, pendulous breasts, they'd been hanging before his eyes, layering sadness and guilt over the excitement of lust. But these were small, up tilting; they gave him lust only, and it was simple and thrilling.

The nipples stared out like eyes. Then the man's head moved down, covering them as he fitted one in his mouth. Jasper was explaining that there was probably no milk because the woman didn't have kids, but Sam didn't hear him. He was too filled with sensation. The man took off his jacket, his shirt, stepped out of his pants, his buttocks as pale as two moons, and then walked to the doorway and flicked the light switch that made the room go black.

"Oh man," Jasper cried, "oh man!" He rolled onto the ground next to Sam.

A cricket's song opened the night. A breeze brushed Jasper's face, and his shirt lay hot and heavy on his chest. He pulled it over his head, and when the fabric touched his mouth, it woke up his lips, and then his scalp as the cotton band around the neckline circled it.

"What are you doing?"

Flinging the shirt down, Sam thought the answer was pretty obvious. He touched his own narrow, hairless chest, his fingers finding his flat brown nipples and sending a shot of heat inward. "Do it," he whispered.

And of course Jasper replied with the very question he dreaded. "Do what?"

But as Sam's lips were moving in close to touch the spider web softness of Jasper's face, Jasper's hand grabbed the solid lump in Sam's pants.

For once, when they parted at Jasper's house later that night, Jasper didn't say, "Aren't you glad we did this?" Only, "See you," two blessedly neutral words tossed carelessly into the atmosphere.

The next day, Sam rode past Jasper's after lunch. The van was gone and the garage doors were closed. For the last week, Mrs. Sims had been talking about taking Jasper and Emily up to Rochester to go school shopping, and Sam figured that was where they went. A trip to Rochester would take the whole day, so Sam decided he would simply do by himself the thing he wanted to do with Jasper. It was a plan of sorts, though he hadn't bothered to think past the first step.

It was the last week of summer vacation. Some of the maples had started to turn, and insects whined in the weeds along 417 as Sam biked to the village. A pickup sped past, then shimmered in the distance. He rode to Second Street and slowed down at the house where everything had happened the night before. In the daytime, the blank windows seemed no different than any of the others. The Pontiac was back in the driveway, and he wondered when it had returned. He noticed a clothesline in the backyard that he hadn't seen in the dark and saw a metal table with a ragged looking umbrella over it. He rode to the end of the block, turned around, and rode past the house again. At the other end, he got off his bike and stood in the shade under a tree, figuring out his first move. Then he rolled his bike down the sidewalk and left it at the end of the walk-way to number 7.

His footsteps on the wooden slats of the porch were so loud he wondered if someone in the house were hearing them al-ready. Through the screen, he could see a hallway. There were voices, a clatter of dishes, and picturing the mess in the kitchen, he rapped at the wooden frame. "Hello?"

The voices stopped. He rapped again, called, "Anybody home?"

Then she was there. Skin just on the other side of the screen, hair. All he had wanted was to see what she looked like up close. But now that she was in front of him, he realized he couldn't just look. He had to say something. Even though she was not what he expected. She was not soft and shapely; her mouth was not hun-gry. Instead, her face was closed and hard, her body was stiff, and she looked at him in an unfriendly way. He could see him-self in her eyes, a boy with a dirty neck and a torn shirt.

"Yes?"

She had no interest in him at all. That didn't seem fair when he had so much interest in her.

"Can I help you?"

Thin dark eyebrows arched over green eyes. Her face was heart shaped and very pale, and her brown hair, falling around it, was curly. She might have been pretty if her lips could have smiled, but they were pressed together, flattened out. "What do you want?"

"Mrs. Sparrow?" he asked.

"There's no Mrs. Sparrow here."

"Sorry to bother you," he mumbled, and began to walk away, but he could feel her still standing there to make sure he really left, so he turned around. Her hand was on her waist and she had on a pair of very short shorts that showed her thin, pale legs. "Do you know which house is hers?"

"Mrs. Sparrow?" Her lips went even flatter. "There's no Mrs. Sparrow around here."

"Sorry," he said. Then he added, because he didn't want her to go away: "Number seven, Second Street, that's what they told me."

"Who told you?"

"Down to the supermarket. There's a delivery. She can't pick it up herself because she's old. Would your boyfriend know?"

"My boyfriend?" she asked in disbelief. "Who are you?"

"Sam."

"Sam who?"

"Sam Smith."

"You need to get off my porch and hop onto your little bicycle out there and quit bothering me. Understand?"

"Yes ma'am. Sorry for the inconvenience." He thought she'd close the big solid door then, but she didn't. He could feel her watching as he picked his bicycle off the ground, sending hate and meanness through the screen. Well, she was lucky. He could have said, "I saw the man in your closet. I saw what you did with him." And why didn't he? Because then she would pull the shade down if she ever touched anyone again.

To calm himself he rode around for a while. Picking another block, he dropped his bike to the sidewalk and walked behind the houses, listening for dogs. It was quiet. But whether that was because there weren't any dogs, or because all of the dogs were napping through the hot afternoon, he couldn't tell. He looked for the places that had kids' equipment outside, because kids meant people had sex, and there were two places, maybe three.

That night when he got to the mailbox Jasper was already waiting. Sam was relieved to see that he wasn't wearing new clothes. It was the same black shorts and shirt he wore the last time, and his sneakers were the same old, muddy ones as before.

"Hi."

"You ready?" Sam wanted to tell Jasper about his afternoon, but Jasper's look made him remember the other part of what had happened the night before, the part he'd forgotten.

"I was afraid you wouldn't come," Jasper said meekly, a nervous smile passing over his face. "What do you think about what happened?"

"What do you mean?" Sam asked. He wanted to be on his bike, traveling through the night, he didn't want to be out by the mailbox talking.

"You and me, what happened."

"What do you mean?" Sam asked in a sharper voice. Why did Jasper have to talk about something you couldn't talk about?

"Was it okay?"

But Sam didn't answer. He got onto his bike, took the lead, and said, "Come on."

The first place they went was number seven, but now the house was dark and there wasn't a car in the driveway.

"Over here," Sam said, and led the way to the block he'd tested out that afternoon. Just as he thought, there were no dogs. They walked from lawn to lawn with no warning barks. But though there were lights on, all the windows were covered. Sam stopped at number 17, because the curtains were very sheer and he could see something happening inside. Jasper came up beside him and they squatted behind the bushes that separated number 17 from the next driveway. They could hear music. It was Frank Sinatra, one of the songs Nelson sang. "My dad sings that," Sam whispered. There were people moving back and forth in the room, so they got comfortable.

"They're dancing," Jasper said, and as if to confirm it, the man held out his arms and the woman came into them. They could hear the man singing along with Frank Sinatra.

I would work and slave the whole day through
If I could hurry home to you
You brought a new kind of love to me

Now the woman twirled. Then she leaned back in the man's arms.

"They're never going to take their clothes off," Jasper muttered. "This is boring. Want to go someplace else?"

"Wait a minute," Sam said. "Wait a minute." Then he whispered fiercely, "Okay, let's get out of here!" He ran down the sidewalk, not caring if people heard them. It was Nelson. He'd recognized the voice. And when he turned the corner, there was the Pontiac parked at a careless angle next to the curb. Sam ran all the way back to the bridge where they'd hidden their bikes. He pulled his out from under the pillars and hopped on. Jasper was just rolling his bike onto the street when Sam was already halfway up a steep hill.

"Wait for me!" Jasper called.

But Sam didn't slow down. It was the steepest hill around there, and he wanted to work his legs hard, punish his lungs.

"Where we going?" Jasper asked breathlessly, finally catching up.

"A place I know," Sam said. But the hill was the real purpose. It would have been okay if it climbed forever. And it almost did. His legs never stopped pumping while the happy sound of his father's voice singing to the wrong woman swelled his brain. His lungs felt as though they were about to explode in his chest, and Jasper fell behind again, so when Sam got to the top, he stood in the middle of the road and watched the flickering shadows. *Fucking two-timing bastard.* They were the very words his father used on other people.

Sam heard Jasper's breath before he saw him. "What's the matter? Why are we coming up here?"

"Quiet!" Sam called. Jasper didn't know there was a house nearby. He'd discovered it earlier that summer, hidden at the end of a long dirt driveway he'd expected to lead to a woodlot or a hunting camp. The first time he'd seen that house sitting so pretty, so solid at the end of such a rutted track, it had seemed like a dream. Nobody was home, so he had looked at it some, then got back on his bicycle, and he hadn't been there since.

There was a good chance the people were going to be home at night, and because they were on top of a hill with no other houses around, their windows wouldn't be covered. Also, he didn't think they owned a dog.

They threw their bikes into the woods and crossed the road to the driveway. It was deeply rutted from the rain and clearly in use, because it was all dirt, no grass.

"You've been here before?" Jasper asked.

"Once," Sam whispered "But we have to be quiet."

From the distance, the house standing in the sea of night looked like a great ocean liner. Every window was lit up, and party sounds, music and laughter, spilled out. There were five cars parked in front of it, and people passed back and forth in the downstairs windows. The door stood open and there were children sitting on the front steps, their high voices cutting through all of the other noise. In the cover of the trees, Sam led Jasper around to the back, where they saw more people sitting in chairs around a small fire. They slipped deeper into the woods, and from a safer distance, put their binoculars up to peer into the blazing lights of the second-story windows. It seemed to be the same room in every window. Pictures hung on the walls, but they couldn't tell what they were pictures of because there was lots of color and big messy shapes they didn't recognize.

The children ran into the backyard, squealing and waving their arms, and soon they were settled around the fire holding sticks over the flames, roasting marshmallows.

"More sugar. Just what they need." It was a man's thick, sarcastic voice. It laughed.

Then the back door opened and a woman stood in the light, looking out.

"Would you like a marshmallow, too?" a man called, a different man than the one who'd made the comment about sugar.

Sam caught her face in his glasses, saw her flat lips pressed together and said, "That's her!" She'd changed into a dress, and it clung to her body as she came down the steps to the group on the lawn. "We're out of scotch, the food's all gone, and Dietrich has a terrible headache. He went to bed."

"We should leave then," a female voice said. "Kids," she called. "We're going home! Toni, can we help you clean up?"

"No, no, I'm sure the children are tired. And you know Dietrich. He has a little slave in the village comes up here to do his cleaning. Worships him. And of course Dietrich never misses an opportunity."

"Can't we just finish these marshmallows?" a child whined. "Please?"

"I'm sorry, but you really must go now." Toni started collecting the glasses. "Dietrich thinks the children are what gave him the headache in the first place. He has no feeling for kids. Never was one himself. Or so he pretends." She was halfway toward the house with glasses dangling from all ten fingers when she turned around to say one more thing.

"She's going to drop those," Jasper whispered. "She better be careful."

Sam had his binoculars on the upper windows. There was a man standing at one end of the room looking at the pictures. Though he saw only his profile, he had a feeling it was the man who had been in the closet the night before.

Now Toni was back outside, collecting the last few things while the guests called goodbye. Cars were starting, and already they could see lights going down the road.

"Okay guys," Jasper whispered, "give us a show."

"She's the lady from yesterday. And I think this is the same guy. Look up here; he has a mustache."

They both aimed for the second-story windows, so they both saw the woman fill the doorway. The man was going over to the wall. He was holding a brush, and then he was putting a big splotch of red right in the center of the biggest picture. Toni moved in front of it and lifted her dress over her head. Then she threw her head back and held up her breasts.

"Amazing!" Jasper breathed.

Dietrich held his brush in the air.

Sam adjusted the focus till everything was crystal clear. He watched the woman move toward the man. The man stayed still, paintbrush moving on an invisible picture. Then a very strange thing happened. He touched the brush to her skin. There was a red spot on her cheek. He moved the brush down her neck, making a long squiggly line. He circled each nipple with red paint, and then he made arrows and curly shapes on her stomach. It happened quickly. At the dark triangle below her navel, he drew red flames. Then the painted woman twirled and skipped around the room and the man put the brush down and sat in a chair. She started to leap. She lifted her hands over her head and swooped. She bent her head and swayed back and forth. Then she skipped from one side of the room to the other and landed neatly in his lap. Dietrich put his mouth to her nipples and Jasper said again, "No milk. But I'd sure like to know what they taste like."

The couple slipped off the chair until they were out of sight. An inhuman cry broke through the buzz of insects. Jasper said, "That's her. That's gotta be her." But Sam hardly heard him, because Jasper was rubbing him in just the way he wanted, his groin on top of Sam's, his hands gripping the sides of his shirt, their otherness pressing into him.

The next morning the sky was a flat, metallic blue, the sphere of sun far away. Wavely was washed with light, the red letters rusted and sinister. Nelson was already outside. Under the apple tree, he'd set up two sawhorses next to a pile of unfinished boards. He showed Sam how to cut the soft pine with a hand saw. The table saw in his workshop needed a new blade, and Nelson said it was better to start with a hand-saw anyway when you were learning the trade. It was hot even in the shadow under the tree. While Sam was sawing, his father began to sink the fenceposts, but the earth was baked hard. His shirt was off, and his belly shook every time he brought the mallet down on the metal stake. Sam watched Nelson's glistening back, because the board cutting wasn't going too well, either. The saw kept sticking into the wood, and he was afraid his father would turn around in a fury every time he had to stop, take it out, and start again.

"Goddammit to hell!" Nelson exploded. He dropped the post and mallet onto the ground and went into the house. A moment later he was outside again, walking toward the car. He backed out fast, the tires sending up a spray of dust. Sam kept on working. Even if the deal were off, he knew he shouldn't stop until his father gave the order. And sure enough, a half hour later the Pontiac came back. It drove up slow and quiet, the door opened, and Nelson emerged with a can of orange soda. "I called Jerry and he's coming this evening with his post hole digger, so we be all set, boy. All set. No sense me splitting my sides over it. Ground's baked hard as cement. " Nelson picked up the boards Sam had already cut. "Allrighty," he said. "I'll work on the framing."

The afternoon passed quietly enough, his father hammering inside the container, emerging every hour or so, his face red from the heat, dripping with perspiration. He left off framing to start cutting into the back end, but the metal was solid and the scream of the blade cutting through it was steady until Nelson's "Goddammit to hell!" broke through the sudden quiet. He disappeared into the kitchen. A while later he emerged with a new sawzall blade and a can of beer. Then the soft noise of Sam's saw purring through wood was once again drowned by the scream of Nelson's. The sun lowered, the shadows thinned, and Nelson left to get another beer from the kitchen. He came back and stood by Sam. "We gonna take a breather, boy. Your mother's cooked supper. You hungry?"

Sam stopped working. He had almost cut the whole pile, but he knew there would be more. The goats were coming tomorrow, it was already late afternoon, and nothing was finished.

"These milk goats or meat goats?" Agatha slammed three plates down on the table. She picked three forks out of the pile in the sink, rinsed them off under the tap, and set out three squares of paper towel for napkins.

"What's this, woman?"

"Goulash," she said, holding a saucepan over Nelson's plate and spooning out an enormous serving.

"You make it up?"

"No, family dish."

Agatha didn't own a cookbook, but she had a little metal box filled with well-used, greasy index cards. It had been her mother's wedding present, and every so often she'd take one out and make what she called "family dish." They were rich concoctions cooked with a lot of oil and salt. Most contained ground venison and ketchup in different combinations with other things.

Nelson sprinkled yeast flakes over the top of his. "Want some?" he asked, holding the can out to Sam. "Your best source of Vitamin F. That the vitamin you most interested in, ain't it? Good old Vitamin F." Then he lifted a steaming forkful to his mouth. "Not bad, woman."

In the middle of the table, next to the tower of newspapers, there was a bowl of iceberg lettuce, a dish of mayonnaise dressing, and tall glasses of iced tea.

"It's great, Mom," Sam said.

Agatha beamed happily. "You both working so hard you deserve a good meal. So what are they?" she asked, serving herself and sitting down next to Sam.

"What you talking 'bout?"

"Milk goats or meat goats?"

"I told you that. Long time ago. Milk goats. 'Cause what this family needs is goat milk."

"So what's Vitamin F?"

"That a man vitamin. It don't concern you. Ain't that right, Sam? See, he knows what vitamin I'm talking 'bout. The pecker vitamin!"

"Well, how you boys getting on?" she asked proudly. She liked the idea of this father-son project. She even liked the idea of Nelson's vitamin joke.

"It's tight," Nelson said. "It's real tight. Jerry's coming and I gotta help Jerry so maybe you can come out there now it's cool. Saw boards while Sam finishes the inside."

"My arms so weak," she said mournfully.

"All the more reason."

Soon as he was finished eating, Nelson went back outside. Sam could hear the putter of Jerry's tractor and then the shudder and clank of hydraulics. He carried the dishes to the sink. "That was really good, Mom. Thank you."

"Is it hard?" she asked.

"What?"

"The sawing."

"Nah, it's easy. Come on, I'll show you how to do it."

"Later," she said. "I don't want Jerry to see."

"Don't you worry," Sam said. "You'll be fine. He won't make fun of you."

"We'll just wait till he gone. Won't take long. Give me a chance to rest up."

Agatha was surprisingly good at sawing, and for Sam the sight of his mother outside, working alongside them, was wonderful. Even though her arms looked like flab, there were muscles there, because she sawed at a slow, steady pace, taking fewer breaks than Sam had.

"Isn't this nice?" she said. "Won't this be fun. Goats!" She seemed to have forgotten all about Wavely, although she faced the big red letters every time she looked up from her work. "I've always heard that goats are very nice animals."

The next morning Nelson went out to buy hay. He and Sam loaded it into Wavely through the new door. It was only a half door, big enough for a bale of hay or a man if he were crawling. The edges were jagged, and nailing a blue tarp along the top to keep out snow and rain, Nelson said, "I'll cut me a proper size opening one of these days. Meantime be careful. These edges wicked."

"Somebody gonna hurt themselves," Agatha sputtered. "Might as well finish it now cause that crawl-through ain't good. Go out there at night, you cut your arm. You cut your head. You kidding yourself Nelson, it ain't safe."

"I'll tell you what ain't safe," Nelson fumed. "Driving a car ain't safe! Crossing a street ain't safe! Riding an airplane ain't safe! You know what else ain't safe? Drinking cow's milk. Artificial hormones make 'em lactate to hell! It ain't nature. No siree, nothing nature 'bout 'em."

The next evening a rusted station wagon turned into the driveway. The door opened on the driver's side and a fat grey-haired man in overalls stepped out and slowly unbent to a half stoop. Hands on his knees, he stood in the front yard and bellowed, "Nelson Sperry!" The door opened on the other side and a thin

man with a dark beard and a flat-topped straw hat on his head
stepped out and walked around to the back.

Nelson sauntered out of the trailer with a beer. But seeing
that one of the men was Amish, he turned around quickly, went
back inside. When he came out again, the beer was gone and he'd
put on a urine-colored tee shirt.

"Got yer goats!" the fat man called. As though that were the
end of his responsibility and the matter held no more interest,
he went back to the car and the Amish man took over. He
walked up to Nelson and shook his hand. "Moisie Groyer. You
know Troyer the chips? It's Troyer but with a G." He laughed as
though this were a joke, his round cheeks forming two red balls
above the beard that was jiggling at the ridiculous prospect of
teaching an English the German name. "Moisie like the capital of
Idaho." He led Nelson to the passenger window, and they peered
in at the goats sitting demurely on the back seat, their legs
tucked under them. "Like I told you, dey cross breed. Nubian
with Saanen. Good milkers. Good disposition. Good milk, lots of
it. Sired by pure Nubian so da kids be three quarters." He opened
the door, reached in to grab the lead ropes, and first one and
then the other goat unfolded its legs and stepped out. The first
goat was brown and white, the next was red colored.

"You take those two ladies right into there," Nelson said,
pointing proudly at the new paddock.

Sam watched from a distance as his father checked them out,
peering into their mouths, feeling their bellies, looking at the
shape of their udders. He talked softly to them, stroking them
all the time, and though at first they had pranced nervously at
the touch of this strange man, they soon settled down and re-

laxed. Nelson left to find a flashlight, and when he returned he peered inside their ears and under their tails, looking for parasites and signs of infection.

While he watched his father with the goats, Sam was also watching the Amish. He'd never seen one close up. They had driven past their buggies on the road, and he knew that the farmhouses with the blue doors were their homes, but the barefoot girl he'd once seen sweeping a porch and her brother leading a horse into a neatly kept barn next to it were so foreign to him he hadn't even waved. The orderliness of their lives made him shy.

Over at the station wagon, smoke curled into the sky. The fat man was sitting with his feet on the ground, the door open, having a cigarette.

"Yup, Nubian with Saanen. You'll be satisfied." The Amish looked at Nelson kindly, his dark eyes lit by something inside his body.

"They got names?" Nelson asked.

The Amish shook his head, laughed a little at the peculiar idea of naming animals.

"Allrighty," Nelson breathed. "I'll get the money."

Agatha came out with him then, and when she saw the animals, her face broke into a smile. "Can I touch?" she asked. Politely, the Amish stepped aside.

"Oh," she chortled, her hand resting on the goat's shoulders. "Oh, what a bony back!"

"Ya, different from sheep," the Amish said. "But good animals. Good animals."

Nelson pulled a wad of bills out of his pocket and counted

them into the other man's thick hand. Then the Amish counted them and said, "Fifteen for da delivery charge."

Nelson slapped his forehead. "Delivery charge? I clean forgot! And the tricky thing is, I'm out of cash. Clear out."

"Fifteen for da delivery. Dat was the agreement."

"Yeah," Nelson said, pulling at his mustache. "I remember that. But see, I thought you were going to deliver them in a horse trailer or something. What you got there is somebody's old car. That shouldn't cost fifteen. Twas a horse trailer, yeah, I'd be willing to go 'nother fifteen, but that's a car, that's nothing special."

"Fifteen for da delivery. I'll take a check."

"Jeez," Nelson said, looking alarmed. "My wife and me, we don't have no checking account. And to tell you the truth Mr. Groyer, fact is that the price of them goats, now that I see 'em, was a little high for my opinion."

"Fifteen for delivery. For Mr. Rymer," the Amish man said, pointing to the cloud of smoke.

"Well, maybe Mr. Rymer would give me a discount. Seeing as I just built me the barn, just bought me the hay, just rigged up the fencing. I'm clear out. Just clear out."

That was when Sam left. He couldn't bear to hear any more. He opened the top drawer of his dresser and took a twenty-dollar bill from the dentist fund underneath his socks. But he stood for a minute hesitating. The voices in the yard got louder. His father was shouting, "You dare!" and the Amish said firmly, "De English always cheat de Amish. I'll get my goats." He was walking to the pen, the leads in his hand, when Sam ran up, waving the bill like a flag.

"Now wait a minute," Nelson warned.

But the warm green paper was already sitting in the Amish palm. "Dank you very much," he said. He opened his wallet and his big knobby fingers thumbed through more bills than Sam had ever seen before. He pulled out a five and handed it and the lead ropes to Sam. Then he walked back to the station wagon. The doors closed, the motor started, and Mr. Rymer drove them away.

Sam watched till they'd disappeared around the curve. Then he turned to find his father's eyes driving into him. "Don't you ever," he hissed, and his hand flew out to slap the side of Sam's face.

"What'd I do?" Sam cried, covering his stinging cheek. Tears tippled in his eyes, but he refused to let them roll out.

Agatha was in the pen with the goats. Now she turned around. "Did you hit him? You sad, pathetic bastard! Couldn't have your son stick up for what's right, could you?"

She closed the paddock gate and went back to the house.

"You owe me fifteen dollars," Sam mumbled as he walked past his father.

"Don't think so!" Nelson called in a loud voice. "That was your choice! I could of got those goats for the price I gave him! That man was trying to sucker me, and my own son helped him along, didn't he? Didn't he Sam?"

But Sam refused to answer. He reached his bicycle, picked it up, and mounted it at a run. At Jasper's house he rode it onto the grass and leaped off, letting it fall. The doves at the feeder flew away.

"Hi Sam!" a voice called from the deck. It was Emily.

"Hi Emily. What you doing?"

"Playing."

"Playing what?"

"Pretend!" She collapsed into giggles and slid down to the floor where he couldn't see her.

"Is Jasper home?"

"I don't know."

He opened the screen and stepped into the kitchen. Mrs. Sims was at the counter. "Hi Sam, Jasper's upstairs."

The carpeting muffled his steps and the orderliness and comfort of the house calmed him. Even the purr of an appliance in the kitchen felt reassuring. It was goodness, safety. He moved quietly down the hall and then at Jasper's door shouted suddenly, "Vice Squad!" and banged in.

Jasper tried to hide the magazine, but Sam saw enough of it to know that the big glossy photo wasn't a naked woman. It was a gleaming, muscular, naked, and hugely erect man that had flashed in front of his eyes. "What's that?"

"Nothing." Jasper pitched it under the bed, out of sight, and looked up at Sam quickly, then lowered his eyes.

"So what's it for?" Sam asked quietly. "You look at it or something?"

Jasper kept his eyes on the carpet. "Only a little. It's pretty disgusting if you really want to know."

"You get hot over it or something?" Sam was still standing. He could feel their friendship sliding away with each question, but he didn't stop. "Like, why do you have it? Did someone give it to you?"

"I bought it. Where we used to live. But I didn't know what it was. It was a mistake."

"I don't think so," Sam said this slowly, coming closer, sitting down on the bed. "You wanted it. Cause they don't sell those things in regular stores." At least Sam was pretty certain he had never seen a magazine like that in the racks at the Kmart.

"They do at bookstores. The big ones. The ones in cities. They had a whole section."

"Like why? Why did you want it?"

"It was a mistake."

"Why didn't you throw it out then? It's like a favorite thing of yours, isn't it? It's something you were maybe going to show me. Isn't it?"

"Maybe."

"But what I don't get," Sam said, realizing that even though he couldn't think clearly, he was marching straight into something he needed to be cautious about, and soon it was going to feel as wrong and unfair as his father's slap to his cheek. "Why didn't you buy one that showed girls?"

"Because I didn't want to look at girls," Jasper said. Now his eyes held Sam's steadily, and under their scrutiny, Sam put a hand up to his cheek. It still smarted. But at least the heat had gone out of the skin. "So what does that mean?" he asked. It was the kind of question you couldn't answer; it was a Jasper Sims question, and he felt sorry it had escaped his throat.

"I'll show you something," Jasper said.

"I don't want to see it," Sam told him. "I'm pretty sure I don't want to see it."

But Jasper got up and went to his desk. Sam could hear him opening drawers, looking through papers. With his foot, Sam slid the magazine out from under the ruffled skirt that went around the bed. He glanced down at the cover, at the thick neck, the arms rounded with muscle, the skin glistening and perfect, slick with grease. He thought of getting up and walking away. But it wouldn't make any difference because he'd have to see Jasper on the school bus anyway.

"Okay, I got it," Jasper said, sliding a drawer closed and joining Sam on the bed. "You know who this is?"

It was a black and white photograph. An outdoor scene. There was a tree, and in the tree there was a girl looking straight at the camera. Only thing was, she didn't really look like a girl, because she had a boy's haircut. But she was wearing a dress.

"I guess you like to wear dresses," Sam said.

"Me? This isn't me. This is my dad. My real dad, not my stepdad."

"Your dad?" Jasper had never told him that Mr. Sims wasn't his real dad. "What's he doing wearing a dress?" Sam asked carefully. Maybe his dad was a queer and that was why his mother left him.

"He went through a stage," Jasper whispered. "Just like me."

"Yeah, but he's younger than you."

"Doesn't matter," Jasper said. "Everybody goes through stages. They try things out. My grandma understood that. Know who bought him that dress?" he asked proudly.

"No, I can't guess," Sam said in a sarcastic tone.

But Jasper didn't notice. "My real dad's mother did. Bought it for him at the store."

"So are you going to start wearing dresses? Because I don't know about that."

"Don't think so," Jasper said. "Wouldn't be caught dead in a dress."

"That's a relief," Sam said, touching his cheek again. "My dad just slapped my face."

"What for?"

"Giving an Amish fifteen dollars. That was owed fair and square. He knew it too. But he slapped me anyway."

Jasper looked concerned. "Is he your real dad or your step-dad?"

"Real dad," Sam said. "Unfortunately."

"Does he do that often?"

"Not usually," Sam said. He wasn't going to have anyone feel sorry for him.

Jasper touched the magazine. Sam didn't look at it, but he could see it out of the corner of his eye the whole time Jasper laid out the next thing.

"What my dad told me is there was this one summer, he was nine, ten years old, and he just wanted to wear a dress. So he did that whole summer. That's when the picture was taken. His mom would only let him wear it at home and only if he didn't have a friend over. So the next summer, guess what? He didn't want to wear a dress at all. It was just a stage. And it happens to every person while they're growing up. It's called experimentation."

"It don't happen to every person. My dad never wore a dress. I'm never going to wear a dress."

"Well, I'm not going to either."

"So where is your dad?" Sam asked.

"My dad died. He was in Spain. He was an architect and after he and my mom got divorced, he was working on a job over there. Food poisoning, that's what he died of, seafood that had some kind of bacteria. And he had a big funeral, he was flown back here. There were articles in lots of magazines. I'll show you." He got up, went to the same desk drawer, and came back with a magazine turned to a picture of a foreign- looking place with a man who looked like him standing in front of it. The man was suntanned, wore a floppy hat, and grinned at the camera like he was happy. Sam could hear his father saying the things he always said about people like that: *Them sort, they think they own the world, but you cross 'em just once and they knock you down and then piss on you. They piss on you long and loud and they shake their dick over your face and with all them drops falling down, they laugh. They laugh the whole time.* Sam thought he looked like a nice person. He had the same look Jasper had, a look that meant he liked you, that he wanted to do things with you, that he was glad you were his friend.

"You see?" Jasper whispered, bringing the handsome smiling man close to their faces as though closer could bring him back to life. "He wasn't a homosexual. It was just a stage."

"Okay. When school starts, I won't tell anybody about it. I promise. They don't even have to know your step-dad ain't your real dad." What he meant was, that this dress-wearing dad, this dad who made Jasper buy the magazine, didn't even have to exist except in that room.

"Okay, I won't tell anybody either," Jasper said solemnly, a relieved look on his face.

"You don't need to worry 'bout that. Everyone round here knows my dad's a hothead. He can sing, but he's a hothead. Fact is, my mother once reported him to Child Protection. They put him on probation. But he reformed. My mom told them that and they left us alone. Which was a big relief."

"Not that," Jasper said. "The other thing."

Sam didn't reply. "Look, there's only two more days left. So tomorrow, want to go back to that house, see what's going on in the daytime? Early? Before people leave?" Maybe Dietrich would be upstairs in the picture room, or maybe back in a closet, and Toni, coming when they rang the bell, would cross her arms over her chest and say, *Aren't you the boy who knocked at my door that day in the village?* It would be almost like he knew her, and Jasper would be impressed when she'd invite them inside.

"What I mean is, about you and me," Jasper said softly.

But Sam, who had the ability to ignore things that caused pain or confusion, decided not to answer. He was already thinking about the next morning, seeing the hill, the bike hanging on it slantwise, the pedals going round and round as his legs, machine-like, pumped them.

By the time Sam got back, it was dark. He could hear the two goats inside Wavely moving around in the hay, their bodies knocking against the walls. He slipped across the lawn to the paddock. The goats heard him open the gate, because first one, then another came out. "Hi girls," he said in a low voice. "How you doing? You like your new home?"

They crowded around him, butting him softly with their hard snouts. He felt their hot breath on his hands, stroked their ears. The red goat liked that. She came closer. He wrapped his arms around her neck, laid his head on her bulging flank, and took in all the stink of her breathing body.

In the kitchen, Agatha was finally tackling the sink full of dirty dishes, Nelson was at the table drinking a beer. The counter next to the sink was piled with the dishes she'd already washed. There was a tower rising up from the drainboard, plates balanced on top of plates.

"You could pick up a towel Nelson, and dry these. I can't stack no more."

"Let the boy do it. He just come back. Where you been, Sam?"

"Jasper's."

"Sims. That's the name. His father work over to the college. Well I'll clue you in on something." He folded the paper he was reading and gave his son a solemn look. "People like that, see, moving in, paying too much for their house, you know what they do, they raise taxes for everybody else. We don't want neighbors like that. Work half as hard as the other man, make twice the money. Plus they get summers off."

"What's that matter to you?" Agatha turned round from the sink.

"He's paid, that's what it matters. Paid to sit 'round and do nothing. Hell, I'd go out and get me a degree, teach me a course if I was paid all summer too. Hell, I'd go join that art school over there, splatter some ketchup at a piece of paper, be set for life. Won't I? Them people are parasites. And there's 'nother one. Top of Lever Hill. The old Fosdick place. Art professor. You ever see that picture over to the bank? That's his. Ketchup splattered on paper. What's that s'posed to be?"

"Here Sam!" Agatha threw him a dish towel.

Sam lifted off the top plate, swiped it with the towel, stacked it in the empty cabinet. "Can I name the goats?"

"They got names. I just named 'em. Sucker One and Sucker Two."

"Nelson," Agatha warned.

"What's wrong?"

"How bout Milly for one, Pat for the other?"

"Them's nice names," Agatha said. "Let the boy name 'em. Them're nice names."

"Milly is a little prissy for my taste."

"Milly is fine. Sam, watch when you take those off."

The stack of dishes was balanced like a stack of logs, and he had to be careful to remove them in the right order. "I see it," he said, reaching for the next plate. Then he picked up a glass, not noticing that its edge helped to hold up a bowl. The bowl moved and everything on top of it started to slide. He grabbed for it, but the rest clattered to the floor, glasses, plates, cups, all of it smashing down with an enormous clatter.

Nelson clapped. "Good move!" he cried. Agatha glowered at her husband. Then she threw her dish cloth into the sink and went to her room, slamming the door.

"Guess you have a little bit of a job there," Nelson said, and he got up and went into his workshop.

When he woke up, there was such a heavy dew in the grass he wondered if it had rained while he'd been sleeping. Clouds crowded the horizon. The aspens that grew next to the ditch shimmered, their leaves twisting in the light breeze. Once he biked away from their house, the quiet hummed. Insects throbbed in the grasses. A hawk swung in a circle over his head, lowering slowly, then shrieking as it skimmed the field. With school so close, even the dry clicking of grasshoppers seemed important, and he got down off his bicycle to listen. Squatting in the weeds, he put his hand down and closed his fist around one, feeling its papery body fling itself against his skin till he opened his fingers and let it spring out.

Rounding the curve, Sam saw Jasper, a long thin shape in the middle of the road astride two great wheel shadows. He stayed still and waited for Sam to reach him, and as soon as their wheel shadows locked together on the road, Jasper handed him a paper bag.

"What's this?"

"My mom packed us lunch. Chocolate, sandwich, water. It's ham and cheese. Is that all right?"

Sam buckled it into his saddle bag next to the binoculars. "Your mom's really nice to me. Thanks."

"You okay?" Jasper asked.

"Broke a whole stack of dishes last night," Sam said. But it didn't matter. With green glittering all around and only the hawks and grasshoppers singing, he felt okay about everything and started to laugh.

"I mean what we talked about," Jasper said, lowering his glance.

"Them pictures and stuff?"

"All of it," Jasper said, moving closer to Sam, his wheel rolling over the shadow made by Sam's bike.

"What? Wearing the dress?" Nelson would have a fit if he knew his son was hanging out with a boy whose father, along with being a snob and dying in Spain, used to be a boy who wore a dress. "That shit's all right with me," Sam said. "How 'bout we get up that hill 'fore it get any hotter."

They left their bikes in the woods across the road and lingered at the top of the driveway.

"Listen," Jasper said. But before continuing, he stopped at the mailbox and stuck his hand inside.

"That's illegal," Sam breathed.

"It's empty. The mail hasn't come. But listen . . . I've been thinking and I think it should be every man for himself."

"What's that mean?" Sam asked suspiciously.

"Anybody sees us, anybody says anything, like if anybody comes after us with a gun . . . "

"Nobody's gonna come after us with a gun."

"It's the country. You never know. People have guns around here, they do what they want. We just run like Hell. We don't have to wait around. We just go. That's what it means, every man for himself."

"Fine, I won't wait. But nothing's gonna happen. This is a professor over to the college. My dad told me. He's not gonna come running after us with a gun."

In the daylight, the house seemed larger and more imposing. There was only one car parked in front of it, but like last night, the front door stood open. There were lots of windows, a roofed area over the front door, and a porch on the side filled with plants. The door onto the porch was open, too. The windows were open as well, and none of them seemed to have any screens. The entire house was so open to air and light, it was like a shell of a house, like something on a movie set. They didn't hear a radio or TV, and insects hummed steadily, the grasshoppers clicking in the weeds where they stood.

Jasper started to walk toward the front door. "Hey!" Sam hissed.

"Every man for himself," he hissed back and kept on going. Sam watched him walk up to the front doorway, step through and enter the darkness beyond. It was odd. Usually Jasper was the timid one and it was Sam who led their moves. But Jasper had just walked across the yard and into the house like he belonged there. He hadn't even hesitated. He walked in there like something told him it was the right thing to do.

Sam moved forward cautiously, staying in the woods, darting from tree to tree, approaching the house from the side, and keeping out of sight at all times. The plants on the porch made good cover. He got down on all fours and crawled across it to the side door. Cautiously, he lifted his head over the sill. Then he went flat and listened. Hearing nothing, he looked again. It was a room like no other he'd seen before. First of all, it was full of color. The rugs on the floor were red and blue, patterns swirling in lunatic designs. The pictures on the wall were like the ones they'd seen the night before through the upstairs windows, big splashes of color, but now he could see that they were women. Naked women standing, sitting, leaning. In one, a naked woman stood in the middle of a country road. She was holding her tits up just like Toni had done.

In all of that color, he expected to see Jasper, but Jasper was nowhere in sight. The rugs covered a shiny wooden floor, and as Sam started across the room on tip-toe a board creaked. He stopped moving and listened for other sounds, but the house stayed silent. It frightened him to be trespassing, but after all the house was wide open, and Jasper had done it and he needed to stick with Jasper. So in the hallway, although he was tempted to walk out the front door, he made himself keep going. He peeked into another room, but it was empty, only a large table and chairs. Had Jasper gone into the kitchen? Along the back wall, there was a swinging door that had to go to the kitchen, but Sam was afraid that if he pushed on it, it would make a sound. So he turned back into the hallway. Shadows filled the other end. It was like walking into a huge spider's web; he simply walked into them and found an arched doorway that led to a little room full of cabinets. The cabinets had glass windows and dozens of drawers of all sizes underneath them. Everything was clean and in perfect order. Had Jasper walked in like that because he figured a man who worked at the same college as his mother and father would know who he was?

The room with the cabinets had a swinging door too, and since there seemed to be no other way of getting into the kitchen, which was the place Jasper must be waiting for him, Sam pushed against it. It opened a crack, enough for him to see a sink, a linoleum floor, a stove. Everything was old fashioned. The sink was on legs and so was the stove. It had lots of silver knobs and shiny chrome panels. "Jasper?" he whispered. The door had made a sound when it swung open even that tiny bit, but nothing had happened. So he pushed it open a little more and gazed into a face looking right at him. Red eyes, the lips in a smile he knew he couldn't trust, the unshaved cheeks dark and hollow-looking, and a perfect mustache. Dietrich. "Come in, my friend. Won't you join us? We're just having tea time, me and your charming companion." His voice was smooth, melodious. "And after tea time we'll have some play. You boys will like the play, I promise. It's boys' play, only for boys." The voice glided effortlessly over the words, and just like Frank Sinatra's, it fell on the air pleasantly and without any feeling at all.

Sam turned and ran. It didn't matter if the man was a professor. He clattered out the front door and jumped down all the steps at once so he could reach the driveway before the pretty voice could catch him. The driveway was freedom and at the end of it, across the road, his bike was right where he left it. And Jasper's was right there next to it. How good it was to grip the sturdy metal handlebars. He wheeled it out to the road, and waited for Jasper to get loose. But after a while it seemed clear that he wasn't coming, so Sam hid the bike again, went down the driveway, and crept through the woods back to the house. The front door was still open, the side door was still open, and there weren't any sounds. No one was screaming. No one was being slapped or beaten. There were no sounds of breakage.

He squatted down in the shadows and waited. Ants got into his socks. So he stood up and shook his legs out, and staying in the woods, crept around to the back of the house, where he stopped in surprise. In the darkness of the night before he hadn't seen the flowerbeds or the brick walks or the neatly clipped bushes. There were tall red blossoms full of bees next to pink blossoms that smelled very sweet.

The windows into the kitchen were open too, no screens in them either, making inside and outside the same. So he was almost inside with Jasper, he just happened to be on the other side of the wall, but he was listening, watching, protecting his friend. The minute he heard something, a cry, a slap, he'd run for his bike and get help. Next to the window something caught his eye. The sun was striking a quick flashing movement. That's when he saw the pool in the middle of the terrace. But not for swimming. It was too small and narrow for that. Fluorescent orange fish shimmied through the dark water, their scales glittering in the light. Sam edged closer.

He wished he had his binoculars. Maybe Jasper was in the upstairs window looking out, trying to get his attention. What if Dietrich were holding a knife to him? He didn't care about *every man for himself*, he was going to stay there for as long as Jasper was in the house. But the warmth, the scent, the goldfish glittering in the pond, made him sleepy. Waiting was how their friendship had started, when he had waited with hate. Now he waited with something he didn't want to name. It was secret. It was between him and this other boy. Something private.

Even so, the warmth, the scent, the goldfish glittering in the pond, made him sleepy. The backyard was so pretty, and he'd been up so late cleaning the kitchen, it was easy to give in to it all. Charming companion. Play. Tea-time. Only boys. "I promise," said the smooth voice. But he mustn't trust it. He knew how it could trick you. Still, he needed to lie down for a little bit. Not long, and he'd still listen, he could listen well, but he was tired, because last night, after he had picked up all the broken china and dried the few dishes that were left, he had swept the rest of the floor, wiped the counters, thrown away outdated newspapers and advertisements piled on the table, and cleaned the stove. He wanted Agatha to see how the kitchen sparkled and forget about what he'd done. But in the morning, the kitchen hardly looked any better. And with the mess cleared away, it looked even worse because then the imperfections showed, the peeling paint, the chipped counter, and Agatha had stayed in her bedroom anyway.

The sun on his back was as warm and heavy as a hand. He stretched his legs out, rested his head on a pillow of moss, and closed his eyes.

By the time he woke up the air had turned chilly. The door to the kitchen was shut. The windows were closed too, the window glass black and shiny, rippled with the light of late afternoon. Sam woke with a feeling that something was wrong. He scrambled to his feet, and when he got to the road his heart was beating loudly. But his bicycle was still there. It hadn't been touched, though the back tire was almost flat. Jasper's was gone. So he sped down the dirt road, going much too fast for such a steep descent, skidding and swerving on the dead tire, destroying his back rim.

At Jasper's house, the bike was propped against the garage. Sam ran onto the porch and peered in. They were all seated at the kitchen table eating dinner. When he rapped on the door, Jasper looked up, said something to his mother, and walked across the living room.

"Hi," he said. But he didn't open the door, just stood on the other side of it, looking out past Sam's head.

"I waited for you," Sam whispered. "I fell asleep waiting for you. You saw my bike. Why'd you leave?"

"We're having dinner," Jasper said at regular volume.

"So what happened? Was Toni there?"

Mrs. Sims called out, "Ask Sam to join us for dinner," but Jasper turned around and said, "He's already eaten." Then he whispered, "Gotta go."

"I'll be at the mailbox. Ten o'clock!"

At his house everything was dark. The car was gone. Agatha's bedroom door was open, her bed empty. Then Sam remembered it was Monday night, the Hootenanny. He looked for something to eat in the refrigerator, and finding nothing, shook saltines out of the box sitting on the table and dipped them into the yeast flakes. Vitamin F. Then he got on his bike and pedaled furiously all the way to Wellsville.

He got there just in time. People were moving from the re-freshment table to their seats, but Nelson was nowhere in sight. Agatha waved him over to the empty place next to her. "I was hoping you'd show up. Where you been?"

"Jasper's."

"That's nice," she said automatically, her eyes clouding over.

"I'm really sorry 'bout last night, Mom. Did you see how I cleaned up?"

"You sweet boy, everything was so beautiful looking!" She pat-ted his knee. "And I'm so glad . . . "

But Nelson walked across the front of the room right then and blew into the mike. The buzz of conversation stopped. The last people clattered into seats. His father was wearing a pair of light blue corduroy pants Sam had never seen before, and his cowboy boots gleamed with fresh polish.

"Howdy folks," he crooned. "Glad you all could make it. I'm going to start the night off with a new song for you all's enjoy- ment. I got me a pair of beautiful girls yesterday. Goats. Cross of Saanen and Nubian. Prettiest little darlings go by the names of Milly and Pat." He winked at Sam. "And there's another pretty woman in my life, sitting right over there with my son. Well, this little ditty's in celebration of all the beautiful women in the world, God knows we'd be lost without 'em, but I gotta warn you, if you ain't got a sense of humor, if you don't love life and all the best things in it, and if you don't like your lyrics be a little spice and heat, well, this song might not be for you. But if you love life and what do I mean by that you wonder, well this little song gonna tell you. Let's just say I hope none of you all's a prude." He beamed, looked them over like a minister in a church might look at his congregation, and began to sing the song Sam had heard the other day.

And that's why birds do it, bees do it
Even educated fleas do it
Let's do it, let's fall in love.

When he got to *Roosters do it with a doodle and cock* there were hoots and hollers, and when it was over they gave enormous ap- plause.

"Well that's a hard act to follow," said Earl Gibbons, the owner of the feed store and the next man in the row of performers. "But I'll do my best." He moved the mike over to his seat and, picking a tune on his guitar, sang a popular country song in his thin sil-

193

very voice. "Help me on the chorus," he said, and every time the song came around to it, the whole place joined in.

Sam got back just before ten and rode to Jasper's mailbox. His friend wasn't there. Seeing a light on in the kitchen, he tiptoed into the backyard and saw Mrs. Sims inside, talking to someone at the table. Jasper? But then Sam saw that it was the dark head of Mr. Sims. He went back to the road and waited till ten thirty. At ten thirty he biked home.

The next day was the last day of vacation. No one was at the Sims house all day long. Sam checked six times. He went back around dinner, but the cars were still gone.

On the first day of school, he was standing outside his house, wearing clean shorts and a clean tee shirt. It was the same driver as last year, a sour old lady who kept the radio tuned loud to an evangelical station, paying no attention to the children behind her.

Jasper was already on the bus. "Hey!" Sam said, ready to plop into the seat next to him. But when he got up there, he saw that Emily was Jasper's seat companion. "Hey, you're too young to go to school, aren't you?"

"I'm five whole years old," she said proudly.

"Five whole years! Well ain't that something!" Sam said, sliding into the seat behind them. "Jas," he whispered.

But Jasper didn't turn around.

"Whatsa matter?"

Now Jasper did turn around. But his expression was chilly, and he wouldn't look Sam in the eye as he said, "I wish for once you would quit bothering me, okay?"

"Yeah, but . . . "

"But nothing," Jasper hissed. He looked straight ahead till they got to school, and then he took Emily's hand and filed out without waiting for Sam.

They were in different homerooms, but two of their classes were together, and at lunch Sam sat across from him.

"We got the goats. Did I tell you?"

"Yes, you did."

"Milly and Pat. I named them. They're going to have their kids in February."

"Whoopee," Jasper said.

"I get it," Sam said slowly. "It's okay being friends with the deer cutter's son in the summer, but once school starts, you not gonna be caught dead talking to trash like him. That's it, ain't it? You lousy, rich, city bastard."

Jasper didn't say anything. He just put all his food on the tray, walked it over to the kitchen, and went out of the cafeteria.

At the end of the day, Sam got off at Jasper's stop, and before he could go into the house he grabbed his arm. He'd been thinking about what he'd blurted out at lunch, and he'd decided that Jasper wasn't a snob at all, that the brush-off had to do with Dietrich and the house at the top of the hill. It had to do with the painted woman, too. And their fumbling at each other in the dark. It had to do with all of those things. The magazine, plus the fact that Jasper's father used to wear a dress and then died and Sam's father didn't. It was a big, complicated mess, and the only messes Sam had experience with were the simple ones that got cleaned up with angry voices, a slap on the face, or a sink full of dish soap. At the top of this complication was his worry about what the man had done to Jasper in the house. Maybe it was the same stuff as in that magazine, but how could he even ask such a question?

So what Sam said, when he caught Jasper by the arm as the school bus rattled past, was the only word he knew that might cancel out the frightened, impatient look on Jasper's face. "Sorry." He had to shout it because the bus drowned out everything. But Jasper heard; he could feel him relax. "For what?" he asked in the old voice. He was looking straight at him. Sam kept his eyes on his friend's face and said, "For whatever happened up there."

And he knew Jasper knew what he meant by up there, knew it made a difference, because Jasper said, "Thanks. Thanks a lot." He almost smiled; his straight shiny teeth glittered in the autumn sun. But then his mouth slipped down and dropped at an ugly, crooked slant, hanging wide open with all the darkness inside it visible, and a sudden involuntary tremor on his lips. Sam watched in horror as Jasper tried to gain control. When he did, when his face was as calm and opinionated as on the very first day they talked, Sam ignored what he had just seen and asked, "So what happened?"

But it was too soon. He saw that right away. And he also knew, though he wouldn't have been able to find the way to say this, that it wasn't a fair question, because every time that summer when Jasper had wanted to talk about what they did together, Sam had ignored him. So just as Sam had learned to speak about things he never would have spoken about before, Jasper had learned to clam up when the subject was boys touching each other. "Maybe later," he mumbled, looking down at the ground. Then he pulled his arm out of Sam's grip and walked up to his porch.

"Like when?" Sam shouted. But he knew the answer. Jasper was on the porch; he was in the road, and the same clay soil that generations of his family had stood on was hard and rutted under his shoes. And it would be under his shoes for his whole life, while Jasper's shoes could walk away from it.

That winter brought unexpected things. Nelson moved out. Agatha said he was living with a slut in the village and as far as she was concerned, the lady could have him. She did the deer cutting all by herself, with Sam helping after school. He shot two doe for their freezer, so they had plenty to eat, but with helping his mother in the barn and going out hunting, his schoolwork suffered and he failed two classes. The season wore his mother out, and once it ended in December she stayed in her room even more. The only good things that happened were the births that spring. Milly had a beautiful bright-eyed doe. Pat had a sturdy billy goat. Sam learned how to milk them, and he would steal the precious fluid from their full udders in the evenings after the kids had all they wanted. Then there was always a quart in the refrigerator for him and Agatha. It was delicious, and it made him feel healthy and full, and three months later, when the kids were weaned, they sold them for good prices.

When summer came Sam was still waiting for Jasper to tell

him. But the day after school got out, Jasper went away to camp and didn't return till the end of August, and it was too late then, time had passed and each boy had grown beyond caring about what had happened in that house the summer before.

Or at least that's what Sam told himself four years later when he was still waiting, standing next to Jasper at their high school graduation because Sperry came after Sims. He watched Jasper's tall, confident figure cross the stage to get his diploma. In their senior year, Jasper had taken all the advanced placement classes the small school offered, so he had a different kind of diploma than Sam had. Jasper got a scholarship at a private college some-where in New Jersey, the kind of college senators and doctors went to. Sam was going to stay on Quigg Hollow, keep doing what he was already doing, which was working at the gas sta-tion so he could take care of Agatha. There was no more deer-cutting, no more goats. A year ago, Milly's teeth had rotted out, and the vet said if she couldn't chew her food, she was going to starve. They could pay him a hundred dollars to put her down right then and there, or save the money and do it themselves. So one cold blustery day in April, with snow misting in the hills, Sam started up Nelson's tractor and, with the bucket he used for burying deer carcasses, he dug a deep grave next to the hill back of Wavely. He hooked the lead rope to Milly's collar and led her along the tire tracks, straight down into the cold pit. Then he threw his arms around her, lay his face against her warm flank, and breathed in her animal smell. He kissed her face, the velvet fur on her ear. When he walked away, he wondered how she knew to stay where she was, but she did, watching him with the patient look she always had, and at the other edge of the hole, he lifted his rifle and sent a bullet into her skull.

The thing he did next was just as hard. And if Jasper ever did tell him what he had suffered at that house, Sam would have traded it for the story of Milly. Maybe it was even equal, because soon as he shot her, the snow grew heavy and the big flakes came down fast. Blood gushed onto her fur, and by the time she fell over there were puddles of red, dancing lines of red on the clean white ground. He started the tractor, bucketed up a scoop of dirt, and lay it down over her as softly as a blanket. He covered her good and then he kept on dumping dirt till the hole was filled. By the time he was finished, his jacket was white, his hair was white, and even his eyelashes were thickened with flakes of snow.

That was the kind of thing you told your best friend. And there was more. If given the chance, he would have told Jasper that it was too lonely for Pat once Milly was gone, but they didn't have the money to buy another goat or get her bred. So he had to sell her, though that was the last thing he wanted to do.

Jasper with his summer camps and his scholarship and his special academic diploma would not have listened to any of it. Which was why, when he watched the new owner walk the red goat into his trailer, the sky, down at the bend in the road, filled with loneliness. It drifted over to the Sperry place like ash on the wind, floating down through the air, settling onto his thin, wide shoulders.

ACKNOWLEDGMENTS

The author wishes to thank the editors of the publications where these stories originally appeared, particularly Margot Livesey and David Shields for their very generous help with certain stories. Most were originally published in a slightly earlier form, some with different titles: *Gargoyle*, *Ploughshares* (two stories), and *The Seattle Review*.

Megan Staffel is also the author of the novels *The Notebook of Lost Things* and *She Wanted Something Else* and the story collection *A Length of Wire*. Her stories have been published in *Gargoyle*, *Kansas Quarterly*, *Northwest Review*, *Ploughshares*, and *The Seattle Review*. She has received a Michigan Council of the Arts grant and teaches at the Warren Wilson MFA Program for Writers. She lives in rural New York.